CW00701763

THE

SINISTER
HORROR
COMPANY

PRESENTS

AN EyeCue
ProduCtion

CELEBRITY CULTURE

DUNCAN P. BRADSHAW

JUNK BOOKS

Celebrity Culture First Published in 2016

Published by The Sinister Horror Company

Copyright © 2016 Duncan P. Bradshaw

The EyeCue Logo Copyright © 2014 Duncan P. Bradshaw

The right of Duncan P. Bradshaw to be identified as the Author of the Work has been asserted by him in accordance with the Copyright, Designs and Patents Act 1988.

All rights reserved. No part of this publication may be reproduced, stored in a retrieval system, or transmitted, in any form or by any means without the prior written permission of the author, nor be otherwise circulated in any form of binding or cover other than that in which it is published and without a similar condition being imposed on the subsequent purchaser.

All characters in this publication are fictitious and any resemblance to real persons, living or dead is purely coincidental. If you think that one of these characters is you, then I suggest you are quite, quite mad.

Cover design by April Guadiana

ISBN 978-0993534607

KEY INGREDIENTS

Adrian Shotbolt for reading this and providing feedback, awfully grateful.

Garrett Cook's Bizarro Novella Writing Workshop, without that, I wouldn't have;

      a, cooked this idea up,

      or

      b, written it.

April Guadiana, for taking a brief brief, and coming up with the excellent cover that adorns this book. Thank you.

PRESCRIPTION MADE OUT TO

Debbie, or 'er indoors, to utter her full working title. How you manage to put up with me and my assorted isms is quite beyond me.

Mum, Dad and Stu, I'm not expecting you to read this, as it's a little on the batshit crazy side of things. If you do, yeah…

To the vapid real life celebrity culture that provides stupid people with distractions to the sheer brutality and futility of existence, this one is for you.

For Rusty Beauchamp, so near, yet so far my friend.

MISERY TV

"Ha ha ha, thanks Ken, I don't know about you viewers at home, but I sure as heck won't look at burned out cars the same way again. How did they manage to get so many dead tramps in the trunk?

Onto more prestigious matters, it's the third weekend of the year, and we've already had twenty-nine awards ceremonies. My favourite so far has to be Ursula Gestwicht, winning 'Best Dressed Foetus' at the annual Cocktail Makers and Chain Smoker awards night, just last week.

She looked just as slutty as her mom in the sonogram, good work Ursula, making headlines even before she's taken a breath of life.

Tonight is the Lou Gehrig's, over at the Roquefort Plaza. There for Misery TV, is the simply divine virus-hound

Imogen Cartwright. Imogen, what's the atmosphere like down there?"

"Thanks Jimmy, I'm downtown, and this place is awash with pus and all manner of skin conditions. I made sure to top up before I left the house, and I am simply *dying* to see who is crowned champion tonight, and added to the Gehrig mulch.

With me is one of last year's runners up, Vince van der Kock. Vince, good evening."

"Hi."

"So who do you think will win tonight? We have been spoiled with some top notch celebrity diseases over the past twelve months, haven't we?"

"That's right Imogen, my prediction last year, has been proven correct. Therefore, I can wildly speculate as to all manner of outcomes now."

"And can you?"

"First, I want to tell the viewers at home, about my top prediction. That at some point this year, maybe even around the holidays, I foresee that yellow will be phased out and replaced by non-denomination specific pastel shades."

"Erm, okay, thanks? And what about tonight Vince, do you have a winner picked out from the nominees?"

"Yes, I do Imogen. I am going to go all out tonight, and put my money on Donald Chump winning comfortably. His work with the marvelous, **Stirring The Shit Up**, was truly something else."

"But Vince, Donald Chump isn't on the nomination list tonight."

"Imogen, I think you'll find that I was correct last year, so that makes me, by default, FUCKING CORRECT. SO SHUT YOUR STUPID FACE YOU SEEPING VACUOUS BINT. You're leaking over my shoes too. Cease and desist."

"Jimmy, back to you in the studio…"

INFECTION

Half past. I know for definite I said half past. Bastard is fifty three seconds late already, this is going to do me no favours. Everyone knows it takes a good few hours for a decent disease to bed in, make itself at home before it starts doing all the good stuff with your knick-knacks and whatsits.

Okay. I'm calm. I SAID I'M CALM. I must be, I'm talking to you aren't I? You're some two-bit, part-time side effect from MacKenzie's **OPULENCE**, which is in remission I'd like to add. The anal sealing has stopped now, which I miss in some small part, but least it means I can finally defecate in public.

One minute and twelve seconds now. Utter bastard. He's done this on purpose, I know he has. Derrick always does this when I'm incubating, he knows it throws my levels out of kilter. I'd check whether I'm sweating or not but my forehead is completely invisible, least it did one of the things it said it would. The ice cream buboes were a little off-putting at first, but aside from some mild sleep deprivation, no harm, no foul.

The price you pay for being a first adopter huh?

Two minutes dead now. Why is he doing this to me? I gave him the number of the clinic where I got my Tubbs Delicious Tumours from, what more does he want? I'm a bloody good friend, he's lucky to have me.

Shit. It's Noah.

Look away.

Look away.

Hope he doesn't see me, such a fucking hipster, plus he's a Stage Three PAPPELS, I *hate* those guys. The wax trails take ages to scrub out of your eyeballs, and my god, when they sneeze, it's like someone has squirted punctuation paste all over you.

Gross.

Fuck, he's seen me, was hoping he wouldn't recognise me without a forehead.

"Yeah, hi Noah, what's up? Looking good buddy, real sick, stage three huh?"

If he touches me, I'm going to jab the antidote in his Casio wristwatch, that'll sort him out, make him a straighter.

Bastard.

Just as long as he doesn't see I'm down with the latest ⌐eila ⌐arraqon, otherwise he'll be all over me, trying to breathe in the snot pollen. WHAT TIME IS IT? Oh, three minutes and seven seconds.

Is that a new testicle tick he's got? When did Noah get that? Thought he was a skinner, what's he doing going and getting a physical? Greedy bastard. Stick to one thing, that's the rule, no one wants to hang around with someone who has the BREAKPKE soliloquy hives AND the Patchy teeth tremors.

"No worries Noah, see you later."

Prick. Good job I can't hear a word he's saying as my ears filed up with alpaca wool first thing. C'mon Derrick.

WOO-HOO, another armpit buboe, wonder what flavour this one is?

I'm getting hints of polystyrene.

Waves of bear trap.

What's that though?

Lurking just beyond the palette?

It's not road tar.

Lime green?

No.

Got it, playing card lacquer. Have to say, although this is definitely going down as a side-effect, it's not been as bad as the Jackson Tampax bulbous nipples. They played havoc with getting my squash handicap down to a nice round five sevenths.

Four minutes and fifty seven seconds.

Ha, look at that prick, must've got an unlicensed Rikkiworm insemination, didn't he watch that article? Everyone knows that if you don't get a one hundred and fifty yard guaranteed parasite, those fake ones will do more than just reverse your gravitational pull. He looks like he's had Aruban death masks sown into his jowls, no amount of reversal therapy is going to get rid of those stretch marks.

Amazes me why people do that, we've got the greatest diseases known to man available at the click of a button, and he goes off to some abandoned cemetary and gets that done. Rikki Carpenter will be shitting in her shallow grave about now. She gave the world pubic jewellery and the second best type of worm money will buy, why go for the bootleg?

Five minutes and twelve seconds past now. I am so MAD with him.

Could've spruced myself up with a quick dose of Stabby's latest little number, something to get me in the mood for a long night of looking like death warmed up.

Finally. Here he is, a handjob short of six minutes. Wait…is he…is he…IS HE?

Fucking joking. He's gone and got the Tarragon too, he told me it was passé, pretentious, but all along he was going for it himself. Ha, he's wearing a hat though, guess his freckles rejected the partial invisibility, that's something at least, I'll be rocking the full lot, and he'll be looking like a reject from last season.

Amateur.

Still though, his buboes look a little less pronounced, and those cocktail umbrellas sprouting from his eyelashes really do accentuate his necrotic pallor. It also looks like he's finally got over the shiny calves from Rita's *Second Batch*.

"Yep, got the tickets."

Least we can skip the idle chit-chat, sure the wool will die back later on, but it'll be good to sit in silence for a bit, nice guy, crap timekeeping, but he is pretty self-absorbed. Never mind, we can finally head to the Roquefort Plaza now, the Lou Gehrig awards on tonight, the pinnacle of celebrity diseases.

I cannot *wait* to see who is there, might even have some free pustules in the goody bags like last year.

What a night that was. Spent all night chatting away to Laura MacKenzie. A true titan in the burgeoning field of celebro-virology. She sure knows her sores from her rashes, and she's good with it too. It's rare these days that you get someone as high up the diseased nervous system as her and still have time for us mere punters.

Rather glad she didn't win really, purely from a selfish point of view of course. She can keep churning out new and improved ways of distending our limbs or highlighting pores with shades of embarrassment.

"Oi! Don't elbow me Derrick, I may run the risk of sluicing your skin off with fisticuffs, but I-"

Oh! Ha ha ha ha ha, good spot, those are fifth generation PENNY'S WRETCHES. I thought they all evaporated into Chinese smog? Awwww, almost feel sorry for them in a way. But still, that woman was an utter charlatan, everyone in the know could see it straight away.

There's no way at all, that you can produce and distribute a high class pathogen without putting your money where your manicured lips are. Nope. As mother always said, if something is too good to be true, then you can bet your scab covered nostalgia that it is.

"DERRICK! Don't you dare, that's your last vial of Hellstones, don't give it away to *them*."

Honestly, you can't show these people any charity, if you give them an inch, they'll take your actinic keratosis straight off your knees. No, they made their mist-wreathed beds, they can jolly well condense into them.

Least it's only a block and a quick step till the bar, get the chance to show off these fresh lesions, bask in the reflective glow of one's peers. As they say, to be in the scene, you have to *be* seen. It's the only thing these vapid disease-mongerers understand, hmm?

My lucks in, I think the ear wool has just disintegrated, not a moment too soon, though it does open up the very real possibility of listening to Derrick quack on about how utterly repugnant he was last weekend. Bastard. I'm certain he exacerbated those gills with rolls of tin foil and pipe gauze, he must have his own stash at home in the septic tank. Only the most dedicated would collect them in this heat.

Bit of a queue to get in, that's unacceptable, but wait a vulvic palpitation, is that Claudio on the door?

YES.

He'll simply die when he sees my forehead, poor man has been frothing at the gums for weeks in anticipation of the new ⸢arraqon release, "Claudio, I say, CLAUDIO…"

Ha ha ha, what a dear, we got in quicker than it took for my elbows to grow back after the previous ⸢arraqon…unpleasantness. As I say, it's the problem of being a trendsetter. All too eager to take our hard earned plastic discs, and not enough time spent testing on the oiks they grow in the factories of theirs.

Least its good honest American oiks, not those imports. Their follicles lack the necessary elasticity to properly replicate Western conditions. Right, just need to get a quick lick of the **YVES BEAUJOLAIS** fly before we head in, this should really bring out the lack of tone in my flaccid shoulders.

MMMMMMMMM. Feel the burn, "Onward Derrick, adulation awaits. Of course, his ear hair hasn't fallen out yet. Or he's ignoring me."

My my, what a sight that is, the ailing and the septic, breathe it in. All that decay, all that scaly skin, the rumble of the physical sufferers in the corner, shuddering in time with the bass. The tangy ripeness of an open wound filled with apoplectic delight. This is my Mecca, the north on my compass, the marrow of my spinal column, "Come on Derrick, let's go bag us a complimentary hors d'oeuvre of callouses."

Derrick and the strange man made their way across the floor, already laced with quiche crust and honey, "Wait a minute!" the man with no forehead exclaimed, "You've changed tense on me, how bloody dare you."

The man with a name, yet not actually named, balled his cracked eyes in anger, "You're just a symptom you know, you can't just change to the third person and expect there to be no ramifications." By now, other patrons had craned their lucid necks to the man shouting in their rancid midst.

"You'll be back," he bellowed over a gaggle of *Perry* sufferers using their warts of Jackie Wilson to do an impromptu, yet spellbinding a cappella version of 'Higher and Higher'. Derrick delved a fist into his eardrum and pulled out tufts of wool. Ordering two tall glasses of bubbling ink, the pair took up residence at the bar, the nameless one attempted to scowl but realised the futility.

Amongst the thrumming noise, Marjory Entwhistle-Fahahey-Ashwin-Lloyd-Burton-Halligan perched on one of her adoring fans. Having adopted the correct ergonomic pose, the flunky struggled to not swoon having the arse cheeks of his hero adorn his upholstered sumptuous back, which was quite enough to make any serious disease connoisseur go weak at the knees.

She idly flicked a spent rollmop onto the floor, the discarded morsel was seized upon by a stampede of over-keen brushes, all shapes and sizes clacked their staffs against each other in an attempt to secure the turgid fish. Her latest husband, Ulysses Burton, furnished her with a fresh napkin, snatched from one of her jovial dilettantes, "There dear, is your hunger sated now? Should I flash fry more peanuts? Just the way you like them?"

Marjory rubbed the cloth over her face as if she was taking

on its scent, before flinging it over the handle of a burial broom, "I require no further sustenance, it will interfere with our love making later, my bowels are still recovering from the cyst removal for my latest concoction."

Ulysses bristled with barely checked contentment and glee, "My dear? Could it be? Have you honoured me so quickly after our nuptials?"

A glass vial containing a ruddy looking oil was retrieved from her thumb knuckle, her posse cooed with raw wonder. Holding it up to the flaming wall torch, the liquid slopped and slurped from side to side, taking on a different hue with every new onlooker. Landmarks and childhood memories formed in the miasma, then just as recognition ticked it off a checklist, it was replaced with another, and another.

"It…it…it's…divine", Ulysses slobbered, straw fingers reached out as the image of the Gefion fountain swirled within the gloop filled glass.

Letting it sear itself onto the retinas a moment longer, Marjory replaced the tiny carafe back in the hand cavity and took another sip from the cup of fresh mint tallow adorned with chocolate sprinkles, "It is my dear, my finest work yet. I've been nurturing those gut cysts since we first met, they are infused with our tempestuous calligraphy and seething desire. The Ulysses Strain will put us back on top, we have much ground to catch up on after the disaster that was Bertram."

Marjory and all of her hangers-on cast a withering look to the limbless husk taking up residence in a pool table pocket, "Tonight, I will release my new disease and claim the Locked In Syndrome trophy as my own. This shall be an evening to remember. If you're lucky Ulysses, we may even get to do it twice."

Her cleft palate winked seductively at her latest husband who had to rely on all of his resolve and morning bran flakes to not dissolve into the tile grout. His lips quivered "I am truly honoured my love." She nodded unanimously, patted him on the arm graft and went back to her drink.

INCUBATION

The toilet cubicle reverberated thrice and then fell slack, the bolt slid to VACANT and a dishevelled alley cat slunk out from the fetid den of inequity and into the bar. The remaining occupant ran sweat and milk covered hands through his crinkly hair, adjusted his sunglasses and bit down on a Mólötöv Mñtε. His veins puckered as the microbes fizzled through his bloodstream, leaving them coated in Royal French flock wallpaper.

Stabby B cracked his shins back into their respective homes and strutted to the sink with the air of a fighting cock. Spaghetti fingers, devoid of bone, tension flicked water onto his rapidly perspiring face, the water hissed and bubbled as it boiled to steam against his skin, "Damn that mo'fucka work quick," he stuttered, swishing his fingers until they better resembled their anatomical diagrams.

By the time he had made it to the bar, his digits were back to normal, and flicking through his pockets in search of a suitably weighty plastic disc with which to purchase a pint of sputum mead and attain the correct level of coolness.

The disc spun on its axis, the images of a gutted fish and coiled oak tree whirled around like an old time viewing wheel, his hand slammed it to the white chocolate counter as his beverage was produced and placed in front of him, "Keep tha change fool," he drawled. His torso did a one eighty flip with elbow tuck while his legs followed at a more leisurely pace. Eyes like plates of kidneys surveyed the bar.

It had got a lot busier since his order of strays had been delivered to the cubicle. His Mite induced paranoia caused his nose to droop considerably, he clamped his designer shades to his face to prevent their descent to the crumb laden floor.

No sooner had the first stringy mouthful of mead crisscrossed its way down his throat, Stabby saw Marjory and her pack of husbands and retinue. He chuckled to himself, downed his pint in an act of barbarism which matched the Tet offensive and strutted over to the party.

"My dear, perhaps tonight when you get to savour the carnal salami, could Phileas record the moment for posterity?" Ulysses asked, dangling delicate petalled flowers over his wife's gaping maw.

Her Velcro tongue wrapped around each flower head with a softness usually reserved for mothers and their young. With a gentle pull and a soft weeping from the plant, the tidbit was separated and cast into oblivion, in-between the crunching of her teeth and jaw, she mumbled jokes from Christmas crackers, letting out small titters between chewing.

"Word up botulism bee-atch," the words washed over the top of Marjory's prostate followers who had formed a mortarless wall around her and her husbands. Her mouth slammed shut like a checkpoint in October, nearly removing Ulysses' hand clean off at the wrist.

"Stabby," she enunciated, spitting a flower heart into a followers tear duct, "how utterly repellent it is to see you."

The bug-thug stepped over the wall and stood before the woman who was bedecked in a crystalline evening gown and matching blobfish eye necklace, "What's happenin'?" he asked rhetorically.

Marjory shook like a burst fire hydrant and showered Stabby with droplets of gloom, sprayed from her fringe, "Oh, you know Stabby, passing time with my nearest and dearest ahead of the ceremony later. I didn't expect you to be here. I thought you'd finally decided to leave diseases to the professionals, and as you so eloquently state on your simply awful adverts, 'got out of tha game'."

"Motherfucka," she added with a wisp of boredom.

Stabby plonked himself down on one corner of the penitent wall, which whimpered and creaked with resignation, "Nah, nah, I'm a been working on something so fine, it'll make your last disease look like it was a nosebleed. You feel me?"

Entwhistle-Fahahey-Ashwin-Lloyd-Burton-Halligan stood erect with a snap so sudden that chaos theorists purported as many as seven Toyota Hilux's spontaneously combusted in Michigan from the manoeuvre. "How dare you, Bertram wasn't perfect, but the source was not equipped sufficiently to provide the strongest microbes. Even harvesting thirty eight percent of his body did not boost the potency."

"From what I've been peepin', Bertram nearly gone cleaned you out of discs. If it weren't for your earlier work with Tony, some say you wouldn't even have got nominated for tonight," Stabby chuckled, pulling out a fingernail from one of the quaking throng and picking out the Mite'd legs from his molars.

"This is a young un's game now, best leave it to us, see what I'm sayin'?" with that Stabby stood up and turned to leave.

"Care to put your discs where your mouth is? Sonny." Marjory retorted with a huff of stagnant dust, Stabby stopped moving, his foot crushing the windpipe of a people brick.

"You mean?"

Marjory floated forwards, her breath left a patch of fine bile on the back of Stabby's neck, "Yes, my dear, I challenge you to a Plague-off."

The *Parry* sufferers, currently reworking Tears For Fears 'Sowing The Seeds Of Love' with a surprising melancholic twist, fell silent. They took the entire bar with them, each and every patron received the shortband text message on their elbow phones shortly after. A wave of bleating and tickles broke the silence, before killing off the eldest bartender with a genital electric shock.

Stabby turned to face Marjory, he allowed his sunglasses to slip down to the hook of his nose, "Oh, it's on, prepare to get schooled."

The bar denizens parted before them as they made their way to a small stage, comprised of two water beds melted together and then inflated with the tears of those who had witnessed the mulching of previous Lou Gehrig award winners.

Stabby got to the stage first and wobbled his way to one side, a spotlight from a portable dwarf star bathed him in a sickly green glow. He acknowledged the wooting and the pairs of void fluid soiled undergarments flung at him, by waving confidently, scratching sores and teasing out pus from gangrenous wounds.

Marjory sauntered to the lip of the stage where her flunky's threw themselves in front of her, forming a smooth, albeit slightly crooked set of steps. Catching her heel on the swollen eye socket of a lesion-maiden, she ripped it out violently and glared at the offender before joining Stabby on stage. Despite the gentle rocking, she was a picture of poise and elegance.

Jed, the manager of the 'Palsied Liver' bar, roly-polyed his way over the top of the physical addicts, their faces tremored with twitches, hands formed into rollers made a runway for him from his office, to the front of the stage.

As he plopped to the ground, an ornate bullhorn, fashioned from melted pill bottles reeled down from the ceiling. He bid for silence as the two celebrities engaged in last minute preparations. Stabby plaited his toes together and then spun them free, whilst Marjory rolled a series of harsh consonants around in her navel.

"Ladies and gentlemen, the plague-off will begin shortly, for those of you who have only seen the officially sanctioned Diz-E-Sports on ESPN, I will run through the rules," Jed lisped, his forked tongue struggling to keep his saliva in his cheeks.

"One person amongst you will be chosen, they must be cured of all current diseases before the competition begins. Each celebrity will then introduce their disease to the host at the same time. The winner is the celebrity whose disease triumphs over the other."

A cackle of snapping plastic and bubbling gland cider rippled through the bar. Jed raised his paddle arms and continued, "Neither celebrity can administer a second dose, so make sure you give them the right amount first off."

Jed wiped a ring of sanitary mucus from the mouthpiece, "Finally, the celebrity that loses has to receive the disease of the winners choice-"

"Bullshit," Stabby shouted, his forearms flopped around like cooked spaghetti, "its award night fool, we can't be going to no ceremony with any old disease."

Marjory removed one of her eyebrows and waved it across to him, it growled like an over-protective muskrat, "Scared are we?" she asked, maintaining an air of maternal supremacy.

Stabby cussed and spat out the 𝐼𝑛𝑓𝑒𝑟𝑛𝑜 woodlouse he had been saving for after, "Nah, nah, it's fine, let's get on wit' it."

The audience erupted in a miasma of Sulphur and potpourri, Jed bade them silent once more, "Let's get ready to make someone, C-C-C-C-C-C-C-C-CRUMBBBBLE, we just need a volunteer from the audience. Sir, you?"

MULTIPLICATION

Ha, excellent, Jed picked Derrick.

Oh, and *you're* back too hmm? I knew you couldn't stay away, good hosts are so hard to find these days. Most are jacked up to their eyeballs on cheap one-day viruses, it's a wonder the whole system doesn't go belly up. Stick with me humble side-effect, you'll see such glorious sights, experience so much aching and throbbing that you'll be begging to stay inside me.

"Go on Derrick, don't be such a prude, look at all of these people waiting for you."

To be fair to him, I would be a touch on the pissed off side too, having just gone through incubation, the last thing you want is to have a platelet cleanser and be, heaven forbid, completely cured.

I struggle to recall the day I wasn't afflicted with some strain or other.

From those early days of knock-off jiggy in the park, struggling to deal with the lactating wrists and sudden sphincter dilation. I almost gave it up there and then, but I saw it through. Wandering through the bedsits of the city in summer, unable to feel the morning breeze as my skin solidified into a one piece sheet of malleable Perspex. That **pi yan so** strain really helped with the personal hygiene, despite the hottest year on record, I didn't need to bathe once. All the effluent and sweat just ran straight off me.

Bliss.

Still, you can't do that forever. If you stay a bedroom skinner, then you'll end up like Thomas. Poor bastard. He swelled up so much that he's now a hotel, the Barkley over on Potato and Waldorf. From what I've heard they get the lesser sufferers in as furniture these days.

Least they managed to find a use for them. And although I rail on Derrick a smidge, well, okay, a lot, if it wasn't for him, I'd probably be a shower screen right now.

Good old Derrick. Found me on the street, being used as a hobo's roof. He sorted me out, showed me that I need to not get too fixated on just one disease. There is a whole world out there of such wonderful symptoms, that it is ones duty to flit from one to the other. Of course if you find one you like, you can always go back, providing it's from a reputable celebrity.

Naturally.

Hundreds got their licenses pulled in the Alphabet cull, a good thing too. Too many were getting in on the act, riding the crest of the wave; their inferior product was bringing the whole scene down with them. I hear most were used as photocopies for the first wave of oik production. They've been copied so many times now, that they've faded away to nearly nothing, a mere stain of their former selves.

Good riddance I say. Kenneth Dailey. Utter wanker. He was one of the disease-boomers, brought out a new disease every month. At first, you loved the mayhem they caused to your appearance. STRAIN FIVE in particular will always be a favourite. Those days spent stretched out as a kite, small children and animals guiding me expertly around the park, and on occasion, amongst the high rise towers.

Hmmmm. I felt like a warrior eagle. Stern of beak and powerful of wing. My prow forever pushing against the head and crosswinds. Truly, I felt free.

But then the infamous STRAIN SIX came along and ended his caper. Turns out that he was using illegal beakers and forceps. His delivery methods were non-union sanctioned, and when they found the vials dipped in ancient manuscript pheromone and promises, well…the council had him impounded faster than you could pop the multitude of blisters that formed on your inner cheek from SIX.

Last I heard, he had been hollowed out and used as a second skin for spelunkers attempting the earth core dip.

Frightful fellow.

"Get on with it!"

Jed does indeed love the sound of his voice, 'look at me I'm a Fall@ws Sufferer who still has the limited edition kimono dragon tongue and ovaries set'. I remember when he used to come round to mine and beg to lick out the used sea urchins from Stabby's first line.

He was a breath of fresh air when he came out. Everyone before was so linear. So faux-puissant and particular, Stabby came along and showed people that you don't need ivory needles, or centrifuges made from black holes. No. You just need a good idea.

I remember squeezing every last drop out of his You Feel Me Motherfucka?, I must confess that at the time, I did not know which end of the urchin to squeeze, it all looks the same. But the moment that congealed mass of ribbon and testimony gorged itself on my innards? Well. I spent the first day scratching so bad that the bones in my feet were quite pronounced. Then the warping began and it was just divine.

Since he started, well, a few have tried, but they all lack his ability at choosing the right method of delivery. Jacob Ming had his scab beetles of course, but they were more gimmick that substance, the metal fingers only lasted what, twenty minutes? So much promise, but oh so little actual end result. I think Jacob services lonely submariners now, appearing to them in their coffee creamer.

About all he's good for I'd say.

And Marjory…well, what could one say that hasn't been said? The way she cultivates her husbands and makes them into something so wonderfully repugnant and vile is quite the feat. Her debut disease, Mark, that truly set the bar high. It made my entire body shimmer like a mirage, I had flocks of lost camel caravans and explorers coming up to me, only to recoil in utter disappointment. I was almost reluctant to move on from that one.

I must admit. Once a year, I still treat myself to a shot from Mark. It wasn't just the mirage's, it was the sanding down of the bladder, the smoothing out of the carotid artery, the lengthening of the pituitary gland. The Celebrity Anatomical and Clinical Pathology board actually recommend that everyone, even small children and used car salesmen, get infected with Mark at least once in their lives.

I wish those Perry sufferers would shut up, we really do

not require the entire rendition of 'Ghost Town' by The Specials as they both prepare. Though it is now Derrick's turn in the spotlight, I don't think I've been this excited for years. Not since I was transformed into a hot dog cart for three days after *Bellino's Folly*.

"You might have to hold him down!"

Ha ha, I knew he would struggle, he's always been squeamish when it comes to a platelet cleanse. I think it's because they have to go in through the teeth, "Don't bite down Derrick, you'll lose a tongue," honestly, I'm a bloody good friend to him.

Now they've got the incisor out, they just need to wrap it in twice cooked bacon rind and stick it on the ceiling oscillating fan to keep it cool, then the small matter of-

OWWW FUCK, he didn't see that coming. Is that an antique watering can? Typical Jed, why bother forking out for a new velvet cleanser when you can use any old piece of crap from the age of SteamJazz.

I'd be screaming too, least it's coming out like a demonic child choir, actually drowning out the clicks and whistles of the *Perrs* morons. "Shut up you bastards, some of us are trying to enjoy the excruciating suffering here!"

I know why Jed lets them in, adds to the ambience apparently, but they just get right on my rotting uvula.

Anyway, I've recorded it, can play it to Derrick later, backwards of course, should provide a suitable soundtrack to our late night water shuffle boarding. Wonder if it'll finally help us discern the true meaning of life, death and saxophone solos? One can but hope.

Oh my. I'd forgotten what Derrick actually looked like when he's straight. He just looks so…well, gelatinous. It's like someone has basted him in furniture polish and apologies, "Keep going Derrick, you're doing so well."

I hope they remember to put his tooth back in after…

Finally, the moment has arrived, they've taken an arm each, what does Stabby have in his hand?

Oh well played sir, "Nice one Stabby, that's inspired." He's got a scorpion, must have the disease tucked in its wooden stinger, I guess he'll apply a little bead of envelope gum to the finger and BOOM, it'll be on.

Marjory has opened up her thumb knuckle, she keeps all the good stuff in there. The tension in this place is something else, reminds me of last year when Laura MacKenzie unveiled the **POST-PLACEBO**. Genius. It made you think you had a disease when you didn't, but you really did.

That paradoxical pursuit of infection really is the reason why I adore her so. I spent a week staring at the manhole cover by Rhubarb and Main, wracked by indecision as to whether I was infected or not.

It was only when I moved and my skin peeled off that I actually knew.

WOW.

Just…just , just, WOW.

Three.

Two.

One.

It's on.

PRODROMAL PERIOD

Apparently Marjory's new disease is called Ulysses, very exotic, she's jabbed the tack into Derrick's thumb and…yes…the scorpion has taken the bait and stabbed him in the other thumb. You can't beat a good Plague-Off. I know you get the ones from the television, but they're small fry. Short term diseases, though the symptoms are a touch on the dramatic side.

I'll give them that.

Plus, they tend to only come from one or two companies, they don't even use celebrities, can you believe the gall of these people? They have the choice between aloof yet alluring people, who pride themselves on innovative infections. Or bland faceless companies, doing it for the money. I do admit to a small guffaw when I first saw the last World Cup, but it really does debase our noble pursuit.

From the spine tsunamis to the flag making, it's all so one dimensional. Plus these companies have the temerity to then start releasing their wares to the general public. Flushed from the wonder of seeing their first sufferer purge their bile ducts in six seconds, Johnny Public think how wonderfully whimsical it would be to be like them. One thing really yanks my sallow skin though.

These ranges of Viro-drinks which are all the rage amongst the youth of today, see them walk around the place with those stupid frosted test tubes. The new one makes them fold into a Sudoku puzzle and pencil, they only return to normal once someone has completed it.

I for one steer clear of those dreadful things, why have cheese when you could have the entire cow and extraction gloves eh? I must confess, I've even thrown a few of the Sudoku puzzles in the bin. That'll teach them. Spoilt brats. I guess that's the problem these days, everything has become so dreadfully commercialised. They take a good idea and do anything to pimp their whore wares out to all and sundry.

Diseases are a life choice, not a way to get laid.

Hmm, I must confess that neither disease seems to have done much so far. Aside from the injection site where Ulysses puckered up like a burst ovary. It's all rather mundane.

Now that's interesting. The arm which Stabby...stabbed...has just started showing re-runs of 'Diff'rent Strokes'. That really is quite spectacular, making wonderful use of Derrick's bingo wings.

"Good show Stabby!"

Still nothing from Ulysses, I'd speculate at this point that her new husband might very well find his limbs being harvested tonight if noth-

FUCKING HELL.

His entire arm just went up like Mardi Gras. My word...that is real life bunting, multi-coloured cloths, raffia ribbons and is that? No, that's impossible, a jazz quartet has formed in the dank recesses of his armpit, they're actually playing 'Tootie Ma Is A Big Fine Thing', that is really rather special. If my tear ducts weren't clogged with ball bearings from this Tarragon, I think these good folk would see me weep like a castrated onion farmer.

See, you can have your throw away bugs, your one and done brain tremors, but this...well, this is the reason why we do this. Why we live the bohemian lifestyle selling handmade chips and carbonated popcorn. Breathe it in, this is culture.

Still seems pretty even at the moment, we've gone to an advert break on one side, and on the other, the band is playing on.

Ha, I didn't see that, a Neapolitan mask is growing from his eyebrows, though the fabric quality does seem a little lacking. Yep, looks like Marjory has seen it and is making notes, ever the consummate professional.

Hang on, what's that coming out of Derrick's neck? It's on Stabby's side…I think it's…yep, it's a muffler from a 1963 Buick Riviera. Not bad, though I do think he's been copying Hiro Takadi from Tokyo, he works wonders with automobile related skin morphing. Remember he did a one off run of a disease, the **RIMJOB** if I remember correctly, which turned people into a Honda Acty.

Not really my thing though, a little too dirty for my liking. Plus it's for those people that are more than happy to stick to one disease. Not for me thank you. I'm a polyvirus man, I like to expand my horizons, not stifle them.

Ahhh, I think I know what Stabby has gone for, Derrick is turning into a drive-in cinema, the screen is now widening and showing what I believe is the opening to 'Dog Day Afternoon'. I know I shouldn't, but I'm rather hoping he wins now, if only to watch it again. Not seen it since I was laid low with the secondary symptoms of that Rug Ting Wing virus out of Chicago. I still get flashbacks to those days when I was a department store mannequin in the ironmongery department.

Ulysses is fighting back, but after that initial burst, it appears to have sated somewhat. The mask hasn't even developed eyeholes yet, that's not going to help Marjory's well-known short temper and even shorter regard for public house patrons wearing gingham. Looks like Jed is trying to change quick sharp, and not a moment too soon either.

WOW. The screen really does suit Derrick, the way it swaddles his ample frame, the curtain trim ending perfectly above his unkempt underwear and wild man forest. Ha, the mufflers on his neck have formed a series of tweeters and woofers, the sound quality is second to none.

Looks like Ulysses is in full remission now, some remarkably unsatisfactory fireworks aside, it's all but gone, "Bravo Stabby, this is amongst your finest work, pray tell what do you call it?"

Bitch in da trunk? Hmm, it lacks something, but names matter little when you feast your eyes on such wonder. Though I wonder what racket it will create in the disease-dens up and down the East Coast. Bobby Temple I'm thinking of you. Crams them in butt to face, so tight that most physical seekers tend to avoid him altogether.

Marjory has gone awfully vibrant and well-looking. I'm not surprised, I dread to think what disease Stabby will inflict on her, especially with the ceremony but mere hours away.

What the hell was that? Sounded like a pack of DORIIA head-butting fiends smashing the front door down.

You're going? Well if you must, go and have a look, I really can't see too well from here and my eyes are going to be reset shortly. Come find me after though, won't you?

An explosion of plywood and particles signalled the doors demise, as it telegrammed out its last rites, it rued the day it was separated from its one true love at the lumber yard. She was made into a series of balustrades whilst he went on to both bar and allow admittance to one of the hippest and most exclusive establishments this side of the accursed canal.

From the doors death throes came the form of a hunched man, as the splinters indelibly worked their way into the index finger cuticles of those caught in the blast, a hush befell the bar.

"You fucking morons. You don't have a clue what diseases really mean," the doorkiller rasped.

Carried on platform shoes three storeys high, with families of pygmy rats living within, the man lumbered through the crowd. As people came into contact with his coat, they shied away, as if they were a stomach ulcer and he was searing asphalt laced with Pepto-Bismol .

Casting a look at Jed which made his skin bristle with a

fine film of spines, he stood on top of Marjory's people steps, and looked across the crowd.

"My god," my host cried out, as his eyesight rebooted, the full horror was revealed, "you're Malcolm McKindy."

With a showman's bow, Malcolm bent forwards, and removed his cloth cap, which released a family of Grizzled Skipper butterflies. They'd been held in captivity since the last days of the Reagan administration, "One and the same. I say, you seem the learned sort, I am in need of a crier, would you mind telling these dear people, many of whom are not aware of me, who I am?"

The unnamed man trembled as if afflicted with fifth stage ~~PARKINSONS QUAKES~~, his forehead reappeared with an exclamation of Peruvian swearwords and immediately began to perspire musical symbols. Wiping away jagged quarter-note rests and bobbly whole-notes, he coughed up a wad of play-putty and addressed the stunned clientele;

'This is Malcolm McKindy, some say that he is the reason why the Lou Gehrig awards were created. He started making diseases in the late seventies, out of the engine bay of a Winnebago Brave. At first they were mild discomforts, rashes that formed from supping on puddle water, lesions that appeared when you listened to pink vinyl. Nothing malicious. People remarked on their whimsy, he was amongst the pioneers of Grue-Wave, those who strived to make infections a collector's item.

During the eighties he came to prominence with his series of what would be called 'The Five Afflictions'. Only when they were complete and one became stricken with them all, could you truly marvel at the exquisite nature of his mind and experience an avalanche of sensations so divine, that Grime magazine declared him 'Celebrity Virologist of the Year' two and a half years in a row.

But then, something changed in him, he withdrew to the outskirts of Nova Scotia, some say that he studied with Inuit shamen to learn their arcane ways. When he came back, he was a different man, gone was the glint in his frown, the spark in his membranes.

The world was enraptured when he announced that he had been spending his sabbatical preparing a new disease, one that would change the face of diseases. Forever.

When the day came, people were queuing in such numbers that the London Underground collapsed under the combined weight. Numbers were limited, for that, we can only be grateful. As the doors opened and a friendly bout of shopping genocide broke out, those unfortunate few got their hands on ~~mad dog~~.

I was too young to see it happen in the flesh, but I remember seeing it on TV that night. The reporter from Channel Pore was interviewing Chuck Randolph, a pizza retrieval operative from Massapequa. I remember thinking at the time how happy that man looked, so excited. He slid the cartridge into his SodaStream and pressed the button. It came out looking like semi-irritated milk. Chuck said 'bottoms up' and gulped it down in one.

The reporter managed to ask 'How is it?' when Chuck's head began to blow up like an inflatable sheep at a Batchelor party. Before he could cower behind the cameraman, Chuck's head exploded like a piñata, showering everyone in a twelve and a half foot radius with dog chews and cheap French cigarettes.

The police went to arrest him, but he'd already gone. Reports say he went into hiding inside Mother Teresa's flip-flop, others that he sought sanctuary on a sheet of microfiche, containing the technical diagrams to the autumnal months.

The Celebrity Virology board went into cover up mode, destroying the Betamax recordings of the events, and erasing Malcolm's name from every High School yearbook they could find. In a few years, 'mad dog' had become myth, the story you tell the ones that are too far gone. They came up with the idea of the Lou Gehrig's, to make diseases be celebrated once more.'

Malcolm finished his Cossack dance and looked at his new introducer, "Not bad work kid, though you missed out my

Nobel Prize for Crusty Lymphocytes. Now if you please, I have come back for a reason. I have such wonders for you all to experience."

An arcade machine crane claw unfolded from his shoulder and reached into a burlap sack tied to a band of handholding two day old gummi bears. A series of whirrs, clacks and oozing ended when the claw retrieved a rusting frost-covered aerosol can from the sack's bowels.

"Now," he cawed, "I just need a volunteer."

The nameless man gulped, swallowing a chunk of energy and nano-yams into the pit of his intestinal tract. Frantically he looked around, watching as one by one, every punter looked away; at adverts for Ice umbrellas on their elbow phones or to call their maître d' to make reservations at the petrol station.

He looked back at Malcolm's crooked banal smile, "It's okay kid, I meant you. This won't hurt a jot." Malcolm's larcenous thumb depressed the aerosol top, coating the man's face in a haze of giggling and cloud residue.

"Watch out for the low flying gull's kid, they have a real mean streak in their bones."

SYMPTOMS

Darkness.

Well that's not a completely honest description. Twas a pastiche of black, a cruel imitator, seeking solace in form that does not belong to it.

Fuck. I'm going to die. That utter bastard. I was hoping my little speech would buy me some time, butter the old psychopath up. All it seems to have done though is make me the first in what will undoubtedly be a long line of quivering mounds of flesh, once solid of bone and yearning.

So this is what death feels like. I thought it would be colder. I also thought that when I went, there would be a bog gas balloon and my multi-toed standing lamp would be waiting for me. I never meant for it to be knocked off that Affenpinscher, his bark was indelibly worse than his bite.

Wait a minute, is that…is that Marty? But…that's impossible, last time I saw him he was being scraped off the bottom of that traffic wardens shoes. After that I heard they put him into lunchboxes as the release button.

Hang on. This is the summer of discovery, when we blazed our putrescent trail across this city; sleeping on the backs of ferries, skating down First on millipedes tacked together with our own residue.

Oh. Right. I'm dying, this must be my life flashing before my eyes, well, if you're gonna go, the most diseased days of my utterly repellent life aren't a bad sideshow before my untimely oblivion.

I'm way too young to go you know.

And pretty.

Pretty rancid.

I've found things growing on me that defy classification, even dear sweet Laura last year said that the pallid tone of my retinas was something that she'd never witnessed.

So, if Marty is here, and we're on Pecan and…Latino, then that must mean.

No. Fucking. Way.

It's falafel night.

Well, let's do it, "Hey Marty, guess who came through for us buddy?" Yeah man, I came through all right, I had to pass

Neil's three tasks of tedium to get the two stools of *Yosemite Park*.

The hottest thing on the street back then, so rare that people were offering two, or in some cities, three jars of organic vegemite for them.

First off, Neil had me paint the disc value onto postage stamps. Two thousand of them later and although my tongue now resembled an autopsy doggy bag, I was closer to my goal. After that, the thirteen hour long rounds of affixing assorted moustaches to passing taxi's and finally describing the wonder and mystery of artisanal Sellotape to his blind, deaf and racist Auntie, simply flew by.

It was worth it though, two crap nuggets with mine and Marty's name on it.

Here we go, off to our temporary slop-pad, on the fourth floor of a derelict fur coat market. The lumps of shit felt like hot dog wieners in my pocket, couldn't wait till we got upstairs. Any minute now, Marty is going to catch his foot on the top step and smack his head into that discarded balaclava, I should say something but it was funny four years ago and…yep, it's still a hoot today, "You alright Marty?"

Idiot.

Ahh, the old place, the times we had in here, if these walls could talk, well, then we'd have to get the building exorcist back in. That miserable bitch really didn't like us getting ill in her old place, remember when I was coming down with the *Full Throttle* virus, which was a bit of a damp squib, those sores were only mildly irritating. She was yelling at me all day long through the light switches, calling me all sorts.

Here we are, Marty will pull the last strands of yarn from his sideburns now, and then we start. "One lump for you and one lump for me. No they're the same size, why would I keep the bits of peanut and charcoal?"

What were the instructions? That was it, use it like a baguette and smear the outline of Papa Smurf on my left inner thigh with the top, whilst simultaneously write a lilting aria on the opposite thigh with the bottom; which had to be about Lois from the New Adventures of Superman.

Marty struggled with that, probably why it took him longer to gestate. What was next?

Ah. Make it into a patty, and consume it medium-rare with a side of apostrophes and crushed cassette fragments, washed down with the tears from a bus driver called Gerald.

Which was harder to find that you'd think. Had to go cross-state for that.

Then, the worst bit. Waiting. This death flashback is going on longer than I thought. Think I'll just fast forward the next few hours, aside from lacing up the packages of jumbled screwdrivers to Paul over at U-Tool, we didn't do much until…

Here we go. A smudge after midnight. The streets are deserted save for two messed up desperado's, as naked as the day they graduated from Bouncing Academy. Yep. It started with my toes, the nails flicked off and little nubs of claw stuck out. Then starting from there, my skin inverted and the scales came out.

Always wondered why mine were harlot red, and Marty's were dungaree green. Mmmm, the sensation is indescribable, I've tried to explain this moment to countless people over the years since, and never been able to convey the feeling.

It's not just when the scales cracked against each other and I flexed my legs, feeling them rasp against each other, it was when the metamorphosis was complete and we climbed up the Wilderness Statues arranged in a pentagram downtown.

We frolicked so hard, I thought my tail was going to fall off, Marty and I ran roughshod over street vendors selling number kebabs and violin strings coated in glitter.

That night…it made me realise that this was what I was, what I wanted to do, and what I would spend every moment of every fortnight working towards. I knew then, that all I wanted was to get as many diseases as possible.

Of course in a few months Marty and I went our separate ways, it's still six months before Derrick liberated me from my rain-protecting life. Took too much, got too far down the rabbit hole. This day though. Wow.

Wait a minute. What's happening? Everything has gone dark again. What is that smell? It's like leaf mulch and kerosene. I guess that is what the end smells like. I've had a good run, if I had my time all over again, I'd do it the same.

Goodbye fetid world, and if you can hear me Derrick, "Stay out of my stash! I've bequeathed it to another."

Goodbye…

"Is that? SHIT, IT'S A LOW-FLYING GULL."

"Ow."

"Quit head-butting me you bastard."

TRANSMISSION

"Where…where am I?" the woozy man asked, rubbing crunchy hands across a hand-ploughed brow.

"You're back in the bar, everyone's gone I'm afraid, the sight of you thrashing around vaguely and crushing monkey nuts with your vanity was quite a chore for them," Malcolm replied flatly, his claw was putting his coarse back hair into dreadlocks.

The man sat up wearily, "But I thought I was dead, that you killed me, that was your plan wasn't it? To come back here and wreak your deadly vengeance upon those who you once called your peers and clientele?"

Malcolm shoved the aerosol can into the man's personal space, "It's my new line, what did you think?"

Rubbing lines of static and Spanish translations from his

eyes, he peered closer at a label stuck loosely to a sheet of permafrost, "**Naturally Nostalgic**? What is that?"

"A disease kid, *my* new disease, I've got a whole new line of them, so come on, what did you think?"

"It...it was magical, I went back to one of the finest days in my wretched existence, Marty and I, we...wait, that was a disease? But why did my skin not glisten with diamond dust or my bones shake like my marrow was being fracked?" the man asked, pulling out a gulls feather from his ear.

"You're thinking two dimensionally kid, this is the third dimension of diseases. If you'd indulge me?" Malcolm asked, the claw tied a length of indigenous twine around his rather fine looking dreads. Still groggy from the reintroduction into reality, the man nodded;

"You gotta remember kid, I helped start all of this scene really, I worked my ass off through those early days when no-one knew what we were doing. The scientists thought the Ostrich Flu epidemic of '77 was nature's work, it wasn't until much later that we admitted it was our doing.

We had grown bored of bit-roles on television sitcoms, I played Ted on 'My Ugly Uncle', until it got canned by the network after they found out that we'd been using an earthworm as Uncle Pete in the titular role. To kill some time we messed around with some discarded swab sticks, petri dishes and misguided mullets. Me and Sam Quentin woke up one morning and found ourselves lying in a puddle of sunshine smelling goo. After paper, rock, scissoring with our hangovers we noticed that each other's faces had become covered in spots which bore a striking resemblance to Josie and the Pussycats. The likenesses weren't a hundred percent, but you could tell.

We were hooked, every night we got loaded and spent the small hours trying out new methods and concoctions. My favourite preparation technique was using a record deck as a centrifuge, but cranking it up to 466rpm, then filtering the liquid through an assortment of greeting cards and even numbered recycling bins. The day after, we'd go out and experiment on people. Depending on what we made, we'd also try out different delivery methods.

One of my early favourites was **Yogi**, we had to get in close to picnic baskets and smear it into the weave of the blanket real good. Then remember not to get too high whilst we watched them run around the park chasing dogs and toy boats around the lake.

Soon we had a commune of celebrities who had shunned the traditional way of life and now dedicated themselves to the betterment of diseases and viruses. In '82 we had the split between the physicals and the skinners, it was good competition though. We pushed the envelope of taste and decency, gently folded back the foreskin of repugnance. By the time I released the pinnacle of my Five Afflictions a few years later, we had it all.

Fame, attention, people hanging on our every distended organ or trembling limb. Problem was, it had gone from being something pure and simple to being the be all and end all for some. We had people trying to get their own piece of the pus filled pie. They'd steal fellow celebrities burgeoning diseases, tease lesions from thrown away soft toys, anything to try and get a few minutes in the spotlight. The dream we had back in those days had gone bad like a Botox condom.

I had enough, after Todd Gunney had tried to remove my latest virus by a black market cavity search, I snapped. The old Winnebago had long since been melted down for infant golf tees, so I stuck out my bestial thumb and bummed rides until my arse cheeks got a rash from yearning for a new tomorrow.

Deep in a funk and having gone untold hours without having some kind of disease wracking my body, a shaman known only as Turk, took me into his Thermos and I began a journey of introspection, soul breakdown and buffing.

Honestly kid? I think I lost my mind.

Using a near forgotten technique known as 'bottling', Turk would force me to smash various glass containers and then reassemble them using wild berries and my innate charm. There were days where I thought I'd never meet the deadline and he would follow through on his threat to turn me into a double four domino tile.

Minutes turned into weeks, into lifetimes bookended only by the tolling of a hand bell. Then one day, halfway through putting back together a pale green demijohn, Turk appeared before me with a clasped hand and a smile birthed from the backwash of a premonition.

My blood and berry juice covered fingers pried apart his, eager to see what I had attained. After I unwrapped his calloused, lemony digits, I saw a small intricately carved crowd scene from the last days of Pompeii.

As I stared at the diorama, I became transfixed by a small gaggle of men looking agape at one in their midst whose head was exploding. It was then I knew what was expected of me, and I slaved day and night on what would become mad dog.

I tested it on passing beeswax salesmen, on their way to a bi-annual conference. Through their pain and suffering I honed the disease, made it become what Turk had shown me in those many pieces of broken shards.

When it was ready, Turk sent a press release to all the major media outlets and sent me via email to his cousin's house in the Bronx. Course this was in the days of dial-up, so the journey was bumpy to say the least.

The rest as they say is history. Like a recalled library book, as soon as the doors opened that fateful morning, I was licked and went into hiding. Each week I'd assume a new identity in a new principality. I'd have to admit my favourite was when I was the underwear checker for Count Hardy down in ol' Mexico City.

Thing is kid, it was a setup, Turk used me so that he could take over the Celebrity Virology panel. He was the one who formed the Lou Gehrig awards, each year taking the winning celebrity and mulching them down into a gritty paste. They say that the disease they make is then distributed to the poor and the incontinent. Truth is, they just release another corporate bug they've knocked up in a cigarette break.

No-one knows what they're doing with all that celebrity culture they've accumulated over the last thirteen years. Knowing Turk though, it can only be a bad thing. That's why I'm back, I'm going to break this motherfucker right open. You see, there's a loophole in the nomination process, I'm going to exploit it and take back what was rightfully mine. I'm going to show the world how diseases should be."

The man gulped down a rusting sheet of saliva, "Okay, you've got my interest Mr McKindy," he rasped.

Malcolm chuckled, a vintage champagne cork was expelled from his waistcoat top button, "Good, I'm going to need your help kid, can a washed up celebrity virologist count on you?"

"Of course, though I do require something in return…"

"You name your price kid," Malcolm replied, his claw retracted back into the varied folds of his clothing.

The potential helper wiped a row of sixteenth notes from his timid brow, "If we do this, I'll want first dibs on your future diseases. I could end up cured and bereft of illness shortly, I'll need an appropriate measure of recompense."

Malcolm nodded sagely, "I can do that, the chances of us pulling this off and not being either ground down to cheesecake base or arrested by the Federal Bureau of Infections is slim. But if there's one thing I've learned during my time as a pencil sharpener for the Raj of Texas, it's that you either make something else into a point, or you break the end off and make them plenty pissed at you."

The man looked at Malcolm with something akin to adopting a tame washing machine.

"Hmm, looks like you had to be there kid, now, here's what we're going to do…"

THE I'M FINE STAGE

My, the Roquefort plaza is as breathtaking in real life as it was in the liquid Marjory swilled around prior to jabbing it into Derrick's hand. It's the first time they've held it here, usually they have it at the Cosmonaut Training Centre over in Chinatown.

This place is crawling with god awful media types and physicals Jonesing for just one more rap to the knuckles with Rattle N' Shake. I hear they take the ligaments from those who succumb and use it in strawberry jelly spray cans to add a little zip.

Are my hands shaking? Or are my hands the only thing that aren't, and it's just my entire body convulsing with a mix of panic and sense of history. Breathe it in, this is when I cement my place in the big time. After this, they'll be urinating my name on historic buildings and tame animals. Just got to keep it together, get through this and make sure that Malcolm follows through on his promise to name the next disease after me and a lifetime of his finest awaits.

Finally, they got round to trampolining the main square, the midget forest just didn't get the requisite amount of pickaxes and Formica needed to get a nice verdant bushy top. Oh that is awful, they're letting those First Generation **Voojets** just run all over the trampoline springs, don't they know that they'll never be able to get the goo out? Mark my words, the City Elders will be re-covering this whole area in gaudily coloured spandex within six days. I just hope that the factories down by the Tusk bayou are geared up to deal with such an order. They were barely able to deal with the beaker shortages after the banana drought back in '11.

"Don't you fucking touch me, or I will dose you with a round of **Salsaria**. Your fallopian tubes will burn so bright, you'll have the local moth population engorge you."

I hate those guys, **Voojets** is the epitome of everything that's bad with the scene. I mean, not even a real celebrity made it, one of those virtual reality ones. If you have no sensation how can you fully master the nuances and flow of a top notch disease? I hate to admit it to Mr Psycho to his face, just in case he has a relapse, but he's right in a way. Something is very rotten at the core of this festering insipid lifestyle. His new line has some promise, I'll give him that, but all I had was a taster.

Then why am I still dwelling on it?

Hey ho, onwards, I'll just double flip over the ready-made pile of autographed test tubes and pus filled plaster gauze. The Roquefort is prepared, I'll give them that. Even the spare moon is appropriately rancid looking tonight, its wan reflection is casting quite a melancholic shade over proceedings.

The spork railings and stretched bovine tongue welcome mats are positively gleaming, okay so they can't compete with the Zero-G chamber at the Cosmonaut centre, but they have pulled out all the stops this evening. What is that smell? Ahhh, it's nine day old gout, they're pumping it out from those giant nostrils sewn onto the Viro-Dew trucks.

Can't stand their twenty four hour prolapse-packs, but their deodorant plugs are something else. They slot into ninety-two percent of bodily orifices rather snugly and emit a plethora of aromas, depending on your eye colour, shoe size and place of inception. Though they are very much a part of the problem. Yes, they took advantage of the market, but therein lies the problem.

Now, if I can just bounce over the scurvy scalpers,

without dropping this bag, then I'll be in business. One does wonder what Malcolm is up to. I'm here doing all the dangerous work and he's probably out back, torturing trouser presses or fornicating with sandcastles.

Eyes on the prize. "Sorry!" very nearly took out that presenter from Misery TV. Look at her, she's faking it, there's no way she can have done as many diseases as she's claimed to and still have full control of her hairline. That's right, smile at me bitch, your teeth don't have the luminous sheen of a viro-hound like me.

Amateur.

Oh, that's not good, they've got the bloody sexy security syringes out tonight. Got kicked out of Jed's a few months back, not before they gave me a bit of a stamping with their blunt plungers. Just play it cool, I'm just a regular Joe, got my ticket and my E-Sports satchel, as long as they don't check it, I'm good.

"Good evening, I must say my dear, your needle is a beacon in the gloom this evening. My ticket? Of course, here you go."

Hmmm, this one is giving me the eye. No matter, stand up as much as my fibrous calf muscles will allow. Puff my marshmallow chest out as if it were a ripe football. Don't look at the weapon collection point, they might get jumpy and wonder what I have got in the satchel, and then…well…I think I'd be fishing myself out of polyp pond. With or without the aid of my opposable thumbs.

What is she looking at? Oh no. I've been rumbled. "Sorry, what? I've been banned? But this is outrageous! I've got a valid ticket, I've done no wrong, I demand access to the arena, now move aside."

Ow, that was definitely a jab to my ROTICULAR tumour, that was finally in remission you know, "Okay, I get the message. I swear to all eighty of the cities bylaws though, that your boss will be getting a sternly worded origami turtle from me in the morning you know. Good day madam."

Damn. I need to find another way in and soon, the overly long and completely unnecessary opening ceremony begins in twenty one contractions. I need to be in place along with my little 'gift' as soon as that's done, or this will be the shortest act of rebellion since the tube sock hippies LARPed against the darning regulations a few months back.

This building really is a charm, those columns of prostitute legs are immaculate, the fishnet is firm yet has a tiny bit of twang in them. The ankle tattoos are really evocative too, the way Popeye is spooning Brutus, whilst Olive Oyl bastes them with Dijon mustard is truly stunning.

Hang on.

I know that ankle bracelet, that's from..."Thomas, is that you?"

It is! Well I never, "You've made it pal, really you have, didn't realise you'd gone full blown and become this magnificent building, guessing you outgrew the Barkley plot?" Not surprised, it was placed among the sacred kaiju lines, he was awfully lucky that he wasn't molested by Battfrig. Half of Chicago is still orgasming from his wandering tentacles and the suggestive fridge magnets he left in his wake.

"No, I'm okay thanks Thomas, just…I don't suppose you could do your old pal a favour could you? Just I'm meant to be in at the Gehrig's, but the security took a bit of a disliking to the way my veins were pumping my blood counter-clockwise. Any chance of a way in? For old time's sake?"

This is my only chance, either that or I'll have to use the roof tassles and abseil my way into the main auditorium. Though my odds then take a nosedive past hopeful and into the sticky lap of a **Hooblly** sufferer with extra puddles.

"Round there?" I can't see anything beyond the wire wool bushes and…wait a moment, there's a hatch just beyond that clotted bunion, "Thanks Thomas, you're the best."

Wow. I thought this place looked amazing on the outside, those awnings were carved from giant set squares and rooved with delicate virginal handkerchiefs. This corridor wall looks like it's been wallpapered with Chinese baby foot binding, look, there are ripped off toenails and everything.

That's a very elaborate looking door, monogrammed with

an S and a B, formed from smaller letters stolen from Jamaican Erotica movie posters.

Should I?

No, got to stick to the plan. Any deviation and the caper will be up. Mind you…I can't hear the musket ball jugglers warming up, once they get going, you can barely muster the energy to scratch your jugular herpes.

Okay then. A quick look. One dart in, nose around and then find the arena.

Nice, this handle is made out of hundreds of nearly expended nubs of rest room soap, it's got real pubic hair in it. Whoever is in here, is someone truly-

"Word up playa, I saw you talkin' to that loco ese back in the bar, I gots a little summat-summat fo your face."

BREAKDOWN

Of course. Stabby B. What an absolute disgrace I am to my family name and snow creation skills. I came to as he was engaging in some long diatribe about how 'da streets' have taught him everything he knows. He's an utter bore, I've been more engaged when I was two days into the **Die Bunschund** strain last fall afternoon. I had the attention span of a dyslexic spoon. Derrick despaired of me, think it was the only time he could honestly claim some moral superiority.

Mind you, this could very well be to my advantage, was always going to be a bonus situation something like this happening. Who knows what dreadful state Marjory is in now, no doubt Stabby has infected her with some hideous anti-social disease. If I was a gambling man, and down the 'Jerry Can Express' on a sun dipped evening, I've been known to wager the odd plastic disc or five hundred, then I'd say he went for **RUNGARDS LUNG**.

No. Got it. **SPICKLY MATASTIC** Heaven knows why anyone would want to willingly have that disease. Ha, remember Noah got it for a few weeks, he swelled up into the surrogate state of Connecticut. The way he birthed New New Haven through his spindly metabolism was remarkable, though short-lived. He spent the best part of tomorrow laid up in a morgue double bed.

He's *still* going on, what was that last bit? Something about my mother being a garden implement? It's true what they say, never meet your heroes. Mind you, he was only ever a momentary infatuation.

Must focus, some kind of side effect to Malcolm's **Naturally Nostalgic**, I think, I'll inform him later. It's ruining my train of thought somewhat. I wonder what would happen if Stabby followed through on his promise to introduce my zip code to his manhood?

Stick to the damn plan.

Right, so, you there, do you fancy making yourself useful for once and help a fellow out of a potentially nasty predicament?

Sorry, I can't tell whether that is you nodding your head in agreement or my neck bone is spasming from the aphid

Mister B had run across my body just now.

Tell you what, I'm going to take your complicity as read, you seem the good sort, so how about, you go and give the little present Malcolm put in you, into our celebrity virologist here. It's Stabby, so you need to use Genome Yak Mesh Three. Okay?

Good fellow, you go and be a good side effect, daddy is very proud of you, making it in this big burly city. I'll be waiting, the bastard has tied me to this antique telephone receiver, I'm not going anywhere for now.

"…and then I'm gonna git the firehose nozzle and it's gonna slip inside your bladder real nice, ya hear? Y'all gonna scream so loud that people in Paris will be telexing you, telling you to shut it, you feel me?"

Stabby B took the time to breathe in, having exhausted his on loan air supply, he did the caterpillar over to a large box filled with balloons. Having stolen the air from a kindergarten classes lungs earlier in the day, he was prepared to deal with the fluctuating oxygen and nitrous oxide requirements his body made of him.

Unbeknownst to him, the side effect drifted around the room, taking in the walls plastered with garish cufflinks and telegrams from Her Royal Highness, the Queen of All That Is Borrrowed. The mirror made from melted down retainers cast a distorted twist on proceedings, the convivial host was trying to maintain eye contact with his kidnapper. Though years of disease abuse had taken its toll on his attention span and REM speed. He'd already been warned that if it fell below 134 blinks per minute, there was a very real chance of permanent rainforest damage.

Stabby opened another chest and lifted out two stray cats, both of child bearing age and good with it. Hoarded Cheerio middles flitted in and out of existence, one, a tabby called Uganda cocked up its leg and licked its bald patch.

"Imma gonna start with you little one," Stabby cooed playfully, ignoring Uganda and opting for the plump girth of Pedestal. "Yo playa, best look at this, then imma gonna fuck you up as I tell the aphid there to give you a taste of Junk Beater," Stabby drawled, combing Pedestal's tail with his bobby pin fingernails.

Before he had a chance to disrobe, the side effect smothered Stabby B's favoured beauty spot and seeped inside him. Once attached to his third ear, Genome Yak Mesh Three was released. It whispered in the recesses of Stabby's mind like it was a mechanic divulging the true price of a service and polish, which was remarkably less than previously advertised.

Stabby twitched, his left sneaker tapped out the morse code for BUY JUBILEE MINTS, THE BEST MINTS

DISCS CAN BUY. As the final dash rumbled through the slinky floor, the nameless man piped up, "So, Stabby, I wonder…is anything odd, afoot in that brain of yours? Something long forgotten perhaps?"

Stabby turned to face his captive, his eyes had formed into a mono-eye, picking up objects which exist only on the Alaskan tundra, "What cha done to me sucka?"

"Not me, my dear fellow, Mr McKindy, well, always best to have a back-up plan, don't you agree? The thoughtful fellow has tailor made something for you, please, relax, kick off your pimp shoes, enjoy the ride."

The world swam away from Stabby like a cheap unicorn. Colours and noises usually reserved for prom queens, bombarded him from every direction, sometimes from opposing poles. It made concentrating on anything above base anatomy highly complex.

Existence contracted upon him like a blue magnet left out on a summer's day, the fabric of reality and temporal yurts buffeted him like a hot air balloon in a vacuum. His vision peeled back and clouds formed from dead skin and divorce confetti lay beneath him like a prize bullock. Bursting through them, Stabby could make out the top of a building on the ground beneath him.

It was surrounded by fields filled with brusque muscle

men tilling burned soil. With each turn of their hockey sticks, clumps of brittle wafer and broken hymen were brought to the surface. Glistening in the reflection of Stabby's toothy smile, they hummed a lilting melody before they were tricked back underground by the overseer, held aloft on the back of a wooden seesaw.

As gravity remembered its role and pulled Stabby towards the desolate looking building, a flash of realisation played across Stabby's pectoral muscles.

"Aww, nah, not dis, anyting but dis."

The sky and hurtling came to an abrupt end as Stabby appeared into the six by eight cell he had called home for three and a half years. As the inexorable feeling of freedom fled his body through any port they could muster, he tamely patted the alabaster wall in front of him.

Long forgotten sensations reinstalled themselves into his undergarments. Running his fingers over a poster of Jed Bush showing the Hopi tribe how to complete their 1040 Sch H IRS form, he heard a panting from behind him.

Swallowing down his distrust of the advice being proffered, Stabby turned his thoughts inward.

He'd been here before.

He'd seen this man before.

"I said, why don't you do my push-ups for me slim?" the man asked again, this time, with an upward inflection on the 'ups'. Standing over Stabby like a prize cock, was the imposing sight of Chester A Duckson, one time PBS evangelical wrestler. He took his vows to the lord very seriously, and dealt with the almighty's opponents in the only way he knew how. By clotheslining the devil in all of his terrible forms, choke holding the misguided and the weak, and elbow dropping the maladjusted.

Stabby attempted to swallow again, only to find his saliva transit system being prohibited by a King James Bible neck bracelet to the windpipe. Chester leant in and took another deep sniff, the colour of Stabby's vest was weakened further.

"Say, I smell evil on you, fish. Best you make yourself useful and turn around, I've got a little something you are just perfect for."

Ha, look at him, Malcolm has worked wonders with the **First Night In Prison** disease he knocked up just for Stabby. As unbalanced as he is, and let's be honest, the man is one runway short of Florida, he has done his homework with this new venture of his.

Oh dear, it does appear as if Stabby did have an awful first night in prison, I don't think I've ever seen another human being used as a trestle table for an impromptu prison cell sale before. Are they? They are! That's wonderful, all of the knick-knacks on sale are formed from his spine and ribs, I don't think I've ever seen a full set of Black Widow false teeth on display before.

Look at that detail, the ridges from the pewter drinks globe are immaculate. Breath-taking almost. It is going to be a shame that I can't stick around and see how much tobacco and long necked screws this array of goods will fetch. For…yes, I can hear the musketeers preparing, time to make like a *Civet* sufferer and split. Though not in half, with a showering of ticker tape and bone whistles, that would be silly.

Right, I've got a party to crash, got to get to the arena, now where's that bag? Ah, there it is. Let's go, "Good luck with the God drive Stabby, no hard feelings, but well, I've got a legacy to create, TTFN."

Ahh, forgot about the aphid, this could come in useful…

THE ACME POINT

Hmm, as helpful as it was for Thomas to sneak me into his innards, one unfortunate detail is that I've got to get through the arena to the seat. Oh my repugnant joy, no. I'm going to have to get through the cheap seats.

Look at them, you wonder the twisted logic the organisers have to allow this assortment of flotsam and riff-raff in here. This event is the pinnacle of celebrity virology and we have this kind of test tube trash slopping onto the floor with their third hand *Billy Two Trees* symptoms and unsanctioned patches of under arm alopecia.

"Excuse me madam, may I pass?"

If she touches me, I'm going to scream, what is wrong with her face? That's tragic, obviously unable to afford **BERT**, I bet she's licked the sweat off a passed out hardworking port hole installer and hoped that it took.

Her children, if you can call the high back chairs with tatty cushions and splashed paint on, her offspring, well, I'm surprised the authorities haven't been in touch and sent them off for genetic redistribution. There are oiks in Wichita who have higher standards than these retches, at least they know their limits, these vagabonds have no pride.

Good job they put them right at the back, the smoke from their fire pits and hollering from the illegal bare gland fighting will never carry down to the front. Now if I can just climb through this monster truck tyre lined with razor blades and Donny Osmond totems, I can at least be free of them.

For now.

Still, it does show the depths one can plumb if you aren't careful. Only takes a few dodgy strains and I could very well be cast amongst them. Forced to bare my inverted lymph nodes to earn a few low denomination plastic discs to try and buy sustenance. Though I know full well that I would end up blowing it all on a knock off vial of SEMI-COLON or worse yet, do a line of *Parrs* and end up being the baritone clicker on Liza Minelli's 'Don't Drop Bombs'.

Dammit, of course, I have to get through the insulation fluid to get to the next section. I hope this satchel is liquid proof, or well, it could get messy at the big finale. Do I tap on the barrier to get in or is there some kind of secret cabal that admits only the maintenance spaniels?

It's at times like this I must come across as a rather sheltered individual, us bohemian types rarely have to deal with such trivialities as wading through a hundredth of a league's worth of industrial insulation gloop.

Fuck it. I'm sure if I can excite this vulvic tube, it will allow me entry. Must be rusty, I used to be able to get subway trains off in mere seconds back in the day. The sound of them panting in the dark recesses of the earth was quite something. Course that was when I needed to get across town to get a new infection. Had to learn the ways in those days, sometimes I could barely move one flattened foot in front of the other, it was either this or I'd take root and become like those other ticket dispensers.

Some even went rogue, the great dispenser uprising in '14 has left a number of stations completely unusable. Cattle vending machines prowl the platforms even now, warding off intruders with lumps of hoof or bovine brain slices.

Here we go, I'm in, though is it wrong I feel slightly cheapened by this experience? No matter, eye on the prize. This will all be worth it when I'm being borne aloft down at Jed's on supple hands shaped like telescopes and binoculars, I can hear them chanting my name now, "-"

Now I've had many things happen to me, but the feel of

this liquid against my leprous skin is wrong on so many levels. I think I just need to find something...ahhh, the skeletal remains of a maintenance spaniel and his guide-oboe. I think I can form this into a crude propulsion device, with just a little tweaking.

Yep, now if I inter the satchel within, I can finally be on my way. I remember seeing a documentary on insulation fluid a few years back. They say that in some places, there is an entire eco-system within, and that the biggest threat to society as we know it is from a small tribe of insul-men and women who spar and frolic in the viscous goo.

I should be fine though, the Roquefort is pretty new and I'd guess that the spaniel died when it became entangled with discarded dental floss and flex. And whilst the feeling is not pleasant, it really does have a pleasant hue, the way it laps over my earlobes is rather soothing. The oboe is becoming loose, I don't think I have too much further to go anyway, there's the exit tube. Puckered like a tapeworm rectum, I think I'll opt for the brute force on the way out, it'll respect me more for doing so I reckon.

And free. It was almost as though it didn't want me to leave, I think I'll keep the spaniel's femur, just for posterity. Heard they can fetch a good price on many of the advertisement poles embedded in central car park.

So, where am I now? Looks like it's the knock off

merchandise factory, aww, look at those little children squeezing those oik boils into those empty light bulbs. Good work really though, with their little dexterous fingers, they can wring every last drop out of those sometimes leathery sacs.

Ha, they're hand stitching human skin handbags together. Waste not want not, that's what I say, if you've been foolish enough to take a second dosing of **GOBBETS**, then you're going to end up with plenty of left over skin. I just hope they've hung them up properly first. My wallet has lines of varicose veins on which came up not twenty minutes after leaving the shop.

Reminds me of last winter, Derrick and I would shave off the excesses from the ones we'd find stuck on escalators or tucked down the back of Arabic display sofas. With some careful whittling and fine needle work, we managed to make a nice line of rather exclusive stationary. The fountain pens in particular were works of art.

Perhaps if I have some time later, I'll come back and see if I can pick up a spare skull or some jellied ribs. I can hear the musket balls being spun dry, I need to get a move on, or any of this expected adulation will come to nothing.

Finally, just need to get through the mid-tier maze of filled up notebooks and I am home and dry. It was a left at the stack of shopping lists, down awful poetry aisle and then turn back on myself as I hit the sheets of historical synonyms.

I haven't scratched for a while, think with all the excitement, Tarragon has burrowed itself into my ligaments and histrionics. Still got to get to the bowling a 300 stage, was rather looking forward to that, most diseases I've had recently have destroyed my motor co-ordination rather than enhance it.

Where now? These pages are filled with recipes for zeppelins and motorised primates, I wonder if I took a wrong turn by the reams of rejected curses.

I kept that one page though, sounded like it could come in handy if Derrick decides to ditch me. Nothing like a cheap petty vengeance gypsy curse between friends.

Hmm, I'm sure I've passed that ⊤⨯-6 sufferer already, which side of his bones were bruised? I know, I'll mark him with a splodge of insulation fluid. The contents of the satchel survived the journey, which is a relief, not sure where I could get another one from at such short notice, not even the knock-off kids could fashion one I think.

Is this a new pile of stick people pornography? I don't recall seeing the stick fisting before…and no, I definitely would've remembered *that*. Okay, so that's good then, oh wait, it's the ⊤⨯-6…and yep, he's got a splodge of insulation fluid on him. Bugger. This is proving troublesome, either I've taken a wrong turn, or there's someone else in here, messing with me.

Now I know for sure that I've seen the chapters detailing the liberalisation of numerical superiority. Remember the binder snagged my leg as I walked past. What was that sound? "Hello? Is anyone there?"

Idiot. What are they going to say? They've been sabotaging my route through the maze, I think they're unlikely to offer assistance and shower me with clues. Wait a gorge rising minute, I've got a plan. I hope I've brought it with me...

Shit, it's a security syringe, and this one is wearing a rather slinky little negligee. My, the detailing in the stretched tendons across the bodice is divine. NO. This is what it wants me to think. Lure me in and before you know it, I'd be escorted off the premises with missing fluids and a sternly worded recommendation for a full body purge. I'm too young to go clean.

That's fine, if I can...yep, here it is, my skin fountain pen, knew I had it with me, filled up notebooks can't stand the sight of pens, this will drive them into a feeding frenzy. If I time this right I can get out of here and hamper the rather alluring security syringe, who is being rather suggestive with her needle and plunger.

C'mon man, get it together, let's brandish this pen and get out of here. It's working! Look at them scatter like white blood cells as the first tendrils of infection seep through the body. Just need to maintain a steady pace and head towards the stage lights.

Is that screaming I can hear? Oh, they've taken the syringe down, I didn't want it to be swamped by them, that's no way to go. "Good night sweet prince," I'll mourn them later, and maybe have time to sneak back and make a multi layered image out of retired spreadsheets tacked together with consulate brackets and chunks of apricot stones.

There's the stage! Now I just need to find the right seat, D26. There it is, I'll just squeeze past these patrons, whilst ignoring the look of disgust in their eyes at my image. I have been through the wringer, that's for sure, don't think I've exerted myself since I used to play little league caterpillar rustling.

Good job the adjoining seat is empty too, going to take me a few moments to set this all up, and then, BOOM, this will truly be on.

I hope that this invalidates the nomination process as the nutter said, otherwise this is going to be the shortest party I've ever been to. At least since my application for concentrated whimsy was rejected on the grounds of a misplaced bowl of misery.

Bloody Derrick.

Bastard.

Right, well, you may as well go and take in the sights, I'm

going to have a brief rest after all that, this should be quite the wild ride. I hope you remember all of this, we are living in history.

REPLICATION

A large pair of conjoined fortune cookies descended from the ceiling above the stage, their grace was eye-watering, even the *Perrs* sufferers who were doing a medley of the Lou Gehrig theme tune and 'Stupid Girl' by Garbage fell silent. "Ladies and Gentlemen, welcome to the thirteenth Lou Gehrig awards, for outstanding services to celebrity diseases, here is your host, Paul Zeckerman."

Everyone in the exclusive Turgid auditorium from the sickly greennecks at the back, through the clacking bones in the insulation fluid, to the fluttering leaves of notebooks outlining the Mexican Dishwasher Peace Accord erupted as one.

Seven new diseases were formed in the first few flutterings, as pus was jettisoned into the air, mingling with particles of crinkly skin and aerosoled mucus. A haze the colour of Maine on 4th February 1932 drifted over the enraptured audience.

Paul Zeckerman, fresh from hosting the prestigious Animal Waste Awards the previous night, strolled into a beam of light formed from a magnifying glass repelling the reflection from a bleached torch. "Hi folks, sure is a pleasure to be here tonight, before we look at the nominees, I'd like to talk to you about adequate dining table insurance. Some pe-"

"Zeckerman. I hereby invoke article fourteen, sub-section one hundred and forty three of the Gehrig Award code," bellowed a voice. With a number of gasps and aisle seat swooning, a second light searched the arena for the source of the interruption.

It settled on a figure carried upon jet-shoes, floating effortlessly over the heads of the whooping notebooks. Volumes one through minus twenty of the 'Avoiding Disaster By Being Dead Already' series high-fived the mysterious figure. Pygmy rats furiously stoked the boilers within the shoe heels. They used smaller family members to mop their sweat and soot covered brows, tirelessly hurling broken-off engagement rings into the furnaces.

Propulsion was extinguished in expert fashion, Malcolm McKindy dusted himself down and strode confidently towards the host, whose wig made from the finest practical jokes of the year quivered, in anticipation, "Malcolm…" Zeckerman hissed through power socket prong teeth.

Malcolm bent low theatrically, and replied, "The very same, regard seat D26."

Zeckerman spoke into his elbow phone and the main light flashed across the audience like an epileptic glow stick. It settled first on a man who seemed nameless, chewing idly on a portion of soft boiled egg-flavour Indy car jumpsuit. As his eyes retracted from the indignation of the light, he thumbed to the seat next to him. A porcelain fondue set, decorated with interview questions, sat facing the stage. Skewers formed from the ribs of primordial aubergines faced each emergency exit in alphabetical order. A solitary lump of stained glass window cheese sat in the ornate bowl, it was resigned to its fate, and was recanting its favourite lines from Descartes' 'The World'.

"So Zeckerman, now I've got your attention, I demand to be added to the nomination list, by the ancient trials laid down by the founding microbes," Malcolm enunciated, his grabber claw idly played with the hem of his scrotal skirt. Another tsunami of gasps and collapsing swamped the audience.

With balled fists and barely checked fury, Zeckerman stomped across to Malcolm, "Fine McKindy, we'll settle it the old way, there's no way you can beat me, my powers and smug certainty will crush you."

The fortune cookie lips pursed and shouted, "Ladies and gentlemen, there are three parts to the ancient trials, first we have bridge summoning."

Zeckerman rubbed his lucid temples with his cigar fingers, he emitted a sound which removed the once popular pastime of straining from existence, and pouted towards the side of the auditorium.

"Ash ma gotty," he chanted until the front row cavorted around the base of the stage half naked with a dart board drawn onto their chests with old burned hair brushes. From the nothingness, appeared the Golden Gate bridge, complete with pissed off commuters and off kilter symphonies which held each support strut aloft with calloused hands and tongues made from crematorium retorts.

As the crowd gasped again, the oxygen level dipped so much that trees four states over felt inclined to abandon their strike over the lack of appropriate childcare and restored the equilibrium.

Zeckerman sneered at McKindy, "Beat that old timer."

Malcolm wiped a glue stick across his chapped shoulders and swatted a low flying baby cloud with his free hand. Adopting the pose of a ghost hunter finding a switch to the play park, he squatted, finger outstretched. As a note in the key of G escaped from his credit card, he pressed a button, seen only to him and tropical fruit.

The other side of the stage crackled with food dye, before a small carriage clock, complete with miniature marching band puffed into existence.

Zeckerman brayed with laughter, beating his chest in time with the syncopated heart-beat of the local monastery, "You've lost it McKindy, what kind of bridge is that?" The audience joined the award host in a series of finger wagging and scalp shaving before McKindy made three of the amplifier stacks explode with the suggestion that their tweeters were made of striped candy.

"Wait till the clock strikes one Zeckerman…"

Everyone focused on the clock as the big hand, made from Lebanese street vendors, clacked and struck the necessary number. With a doorbell ringing in the distance and a myriad of broken calculators repeating 8008, the clock disappeared and was replaced by the Pont d'Aël. The ancient Italian viaduct hummed with the Hispanic only verses of rap supergroup Gravediggaz.

As one, the previously hysterical audience fell silent, even the fortune cookie lips parted, showing they had dined recently on road sign pastries and part time teeth models. "It's…it's…" Zeckerman flapped.

Malcolm yawned, an orphaned jackdaw took the opportunity to escape the daily waterboarding routine and caw-cawed to freedom, "I know," he mustered, "it's divine. Next?"

Gathering their scrolls of foretelling, the fortune cookie lips smacked together, "Next, we have the most ancient of trials. Each of you must extract milk from the lactation duct of the noble Xerox Model 1012 photocopier. Once removed, you must fill four different pieces of Lego with the appropriate amount of copier milk to sustain the Gerald twin mayflies through their retirement. Mister Zeckerman, if you please."

With a pall of thunderous applause interspersed with coughing and dilation of nipple hair, two identical sun stained Model 1012's were brought onto the stage by a chain gang of scantily clad shopping carts. With a flash of highly polished caster wheel and provocatively angled child seat, the carts did the can-can off stage, a number of them displaying proudly the fact they had gone commando.

Zeckerman twisted off the fingers from his right hand and pushed them into dovetail bevels on his free hand. Beckoning the porous crowd for a respectful oohing and ahhing, he approached the photocopier on his side of the stage.

Like a hunchback golfer working the easy slots on the Panamanian strip, he sized up his point of entry. With a vibrant and knowing thrash of his bestial mullet, his hand sunk in-between the keypad speckled with Christmas party semen and pant elastic; and the power switch, decorated with ingots of barbecue tong tips.

His tongue slapped around his pock marked face, seeking holds on the craggy surface. Zeckerman fell still. His tongue, buried deep within an old hub cab impact site, slowly withdrew from his face, tied to the end was the lactation duct, as it met the sweaty and roasted taco air, it quivered.

Zeckerman was now a Human Resources 'unseemly conduct meeting' hive of energy. He reattached his fingers and foraged within his monobrow, pulling out four yellow two by two Lego bricks. Laying them on a sheet of half consumed asbestos, his mullet formed into a movie clapper board, and taking the duct roughly, squeezed the lumpy black milk equally into the upturned Lego. As the last coagulated curd sloughed into the final piece, he ran the back of his mirrored suit sleeve across his old wound which hissed and protested at being abused in such a manner.

"Mr McKindy, would you kindly?" requested the fortune cookie.

Malcolm nodded sagely and took a step towards his photocopier, taking time to notice the intricate go faster stripe emblazoned on its rump. The copy trays slapped together like a bemused paving slab, indicating that it would not welcome any attempted entry there.

McKindy tapped his grabber claw four times on the tip,

and it sunk slowly into the old man's dank muffin top folds, which puffed up around his tightly wound waist. With a tug and spray of gin pheromone the claw retrieved a duelling spoon, last used during the fiendish trench wars of the battle of Hegemony.

Using the rusting bowl, Malcolm rapped the lid, seeking for an egress invisible to unpractised amateurs. As the tapping reached a number eight shattering crescendo, McKindy plunged the spoon through the slightly ajar toner loading bay and ratcheted it around in a Star of David motion. Zeckerman began to guffaw, "You've lost it McKindy, you need to tease it out, the 1012 appreciates being wooed not taken roughly through the toner port."

As the laughing drowned out the dinner bell at the feral helicopter grazing grounds nearby, Malcolm withdrew the spoon and with a speed barely recognisable as movement, swung his unfurled umbilical cord into the newly created cavity. Whipping it back out, he caught the duct at the same time as he slammed the spoon into its undulating teat.

The grabber claw reverently placed four blue eight by eight Lego pieces on the juddering keypad, each one was daubed with a different Jetson character. The spoon gouged out tracts of black milk and slapped them into the Lego. After a brief prayer to the duelling spoon deities, McKindy stood to one side, waiting for the next step.

"You've got too much Malcolm, I look forward to beating you," Zeckerman grunted.

"Bring in...the Gerald twins," the fortune cookie announced, to a burp of excitement and prejudice. A more reserved shopping cart, though still wearing a unitard and hot pants, sashayed from the side, in each hand lay a mayfly, tucked into a miniature sleeping bag. "They've just gone through their mid-life crises and are ready to enjoy their twilight days. The milk must keep them going until they expire, the winner will be the one that recants their Catholicism last."

Both mayflies were placed before the extracted fluid and on the sound of hell kicking drunkards out for the day, they gorged themselves on the liquid. Zeckerman's took his fill first, rubbing a feather boa across his feeding pipe and letting out a pent up embolism. McKindy's finished a minute later, and already it was swaying, marking out its biggest mistakes in a field of crushed velvet, which was caught in a paper loading section.

Therein followed a period of introspection and decadence. Each mayfly would engage the other in a series of frenzied debates and then drink from twelve year old Australian whiskey. Upon the conclusion of a game of knock down ginger, McKindy's mayfly floated to the floor on its back, its legs pulled into its heavy breathing chest. "And now, the moment you lose," Zeckerman gloated.

Malcolm gave him a knowing smile and lit a roll of eviction papers, breathing in the anguish and capitalism.

"I...I..." gasped McKindy's mayfly, his twin fluttered down to be by his side.

As the mayfly touched his brothers flickering antennae, he clutched his chest segment, and waving a balled back leg up at the sky, shouted, "Damn you, I hereby recant my Catholicism. And boating license. Take them, I need them not..." he fell to the floor with a clap of herbivore chewing.

His distraught brother picked up the motionless body, wiped a tear from his multi-eye eye and flew up to the shopping cart's smooth handle. Whispering sweet nothings into her ear, she wheeled away slowly, giggling like a gigolo's palm print.

"The winner is Malcolm McKindy, now the final challenge..." the fortune cookie screamed, "...the challenger must use one of their diseases, whilst Mr Zeckerman can use any of the nominees. They will introduce them to two blank oiks, whichever one is forced to drink from the fountain of ill repute first, wins."

Zeckerman, still reeling from his crushing defeats cackled with glee. The Parry sufferers burst into a chorus of big band hits, as two oiks, fresh from the factory contained within the Saxony bell tower, lumbered onto stage.

At nine foot tall and of a doughy consistency, their three beady eyes gawped at the audience with a mixture of regret and potential pyromania. Their barely formed lips mumbled the seven words which made up their awakening incantation. Legs better suited to bookending time periods of mankind thudded to a halt.

Malcolm sidled up to his designated oik and flicked through his Filofax, stopping on Monday 14 January 1995. He pulled out a fortnight and replaced the dinner plate covered book in his jacket pocket, "Ready when you are Zeckerman."

His face turned up like a set of pinball flippers and he pulled out a four pronged multi-syringe-gun, used primarily for infecting boy bands at the same time with infectious grins and pleurisy. "I've got a little something extra McKindy, not one disease, but all four nominated diseases, you're going down do you hear me? DOWN!"

The fortune cookie went to protest but was met with a punch to his solar plexus, he fell silent. The fountain of ill repute, complete with drinking tube was slung onto the stage by the oik-herder, a posse of sexy security syringes ringed the stage, "When you lose this one McKindy, you're going to pay for what you did to those people, BEGIN."

Zeckerman stabbed the syringe gun into his oiks fleshy knee, discharging all four cylinders at once, as he withdrew the points, he massaged the entry sites with his eyeballs, forcing the diseases to work faster. Malcolm stood idle to one side, he had pulled out a skin pen and was scribbling notes on the paper he had retrieved.

One of the oiks legs started to show outtakes from Seinfeld, one side of its head was slowly being covered in a harlequin mask, still McKindy made his notes. Zeckerman cackled like a broken record player, "You fool, my security are looking forward to clubbing you into disorientation, the things they've longed to do to your hairline are borderline medieval."

As the belly of Zeckerman's oik started to twinkle like the first oil spill of spring, McKindy folded the paper into sevenths, pulled his oiks tongue towards the loudest fire pit and placed the note in its mouth, closing it with a playful pat on its middle arse cheek.

A look of utter bemusement played across its face, as if it was the subject of a Ponzi scheme involving third hand wigs and cigars. A small trickle of gilded saliva ran down its smooth features.

Zeckerman's oik was lolloping around the stage by now, its blueprint being pulled and dragged into four different directions. Its newly formed branches scratched and pawed at its mutating body, unable to keep stuff in or out. A pack of tame kittens ran free from its tail, followed closely by a favourable Trip Advisor review, citing excellent parking and an adequate buffet. It fell to the floor and pulled itself towards the fountain, vomiting with the multitude of symptoms tugging at its nervous system.

McKindy picked his nose and slid out a portable Theremin, as he formed an oscillating wave, his oik turned and plodded towards the drinking tube. Placing an embossed hand on his kin, he drunk deeply from the fountain, before a chorus of wooting rang out from the greennecks at the back, and a polite ripple of appeasement from the front rows which hadn't dissolved with gasping.

The winning oik grabbed his brethren by the still forming cinema screen and dragged him off stage, through the crowd of sexy security syringes who looked on with equal measures of annoyance and arousement.

McKindy passed a chunk of freshly baked coffee bean to his platform shoe pygmy rats, who took the offerings gladly. "My new disease you see, it was in the pen ink, it's programmed to make someone experience a full weekend on the sauce, then seek to rehydrate themselves. Quite elementary really."

"ENOUGH," shouted Zeckerman, "I tire of these games, you shall not receive a nomination, you shall only die. I should've done this years ago."

A hand reached round to the back of his re-tied mullet

and yanked on a zip made from jinxed chess pieces. The visage of Paul Zeckerman fell loose as his disguise slipped away, revealing a man bedecked in Disney tattoos and garnished with the email addresses of MySpace first adopters.

Malcolm sighed, "Turk?"

PERIOD OF DECLINE

Turk discarded the Paul Zeckerman disguise to the stage floor, another row of people melded together into a series of uniform kayak seats. "Enough of this charade McKindy, you weren't supposed to come back, I brainwashed you to remove you from this game."

"But...it can't be, I saw your body in an advertisement for dining table manure. There was even a close up of your ravens writing desk tattoo," Malcolm stammered. His grabbing claw pulled out a lump of the Elgin marble from a backpack, and began to etch its epitaph.

Stepping over his shorn skin suit, Turk turned his shoulder to the old man, showing a patch of scar tissue the exact width of a ravens writing desk tattoo, "I cut it off and grafted it onto the actor, he's dead now of course, had an accident with a parasol and a revolving door. Quite the fool, everyone knows that it's bad luck to go shopping with a closed rain protection implement."

Turk cupped his cellophane covered hands and took a drink from the bubbling fountain, "Hmmm, that hit the spot. You were just a pawn in my game McKindy, I used you, nothing more. Then when I was done, I disposed of you like a chilli coated enema."

Malcolm collapsed to the floor, the pygmy rats clung onto the sideways windows of their abode for dear life, "But why Turk? We could've made such hideous things together. Remember the days after I stuck the ukulele tuning bottles back together, we planned such noble pursuits. Boils which would erupt on the hour, showering the afflicted with Napoleonic era lead toy animals. We spent hours on sculpting the genome for the seals alone, why did you make me kill those people?"

"Because I am...your father," Turk said flatly, the audience gasped again, the sound sliced open the last remaining seal on Pandora's jewelry box, and a number of cursed septum rings tumbled into the possession of a horde of patiently waiting goth rainbows.

McKindy reared to the cheap seats, and roared, "NOOOOOOOOOOOOOOOOOOOOOOOOOO, why God? Why have you forsaken me?"

Turk laughed so evilly that the Axis of Quite Evil people disbanded on the spot, citing their inability to do what was required of them to fulfil their quota of bastardry. "I was joking Malcolm, you were sired when your mother became intoxicated by too many Wine Gums, and a randy jackdaw chanced its luck and fucked her. Twice."

Malcolm hauled himself to his feet, defiantly he grunted, "Yeah? And? Everyone knows that story, my mum always puts out for winged animals, it's her thing."

This rendered Turk speechless, reaching within his casual dictator slacks, he retrieved two magicians' rabbits, which he slapped together. An almighty roar rumbled through the auditorium, as the backdrop to the stage rumbled and split, each side peeled back to reveal a chasm. "I grow weary of you and your intentions, let me welcome you to my accomplice, he will deal with you."

Turk slipped back into the shadow of a nearby hobo lectern, leaving Malcolm alone in the middle of the stage. From the yawning abyss came a whirring of cogs and screeching oil paintings, a bronze spindly leg hit the stage, pulling the rest of itself into reality.

"My god…" Malcolm groaned, "…it's the mechanised iron lung of Lou Gehrig."

Standing around twelve foot tall, with a central bronze body, holding the withered cadaver of Lou Gehrig, the monstrosity thudded towards McKindy. The chattering skull atop the iron lung hummed lecherous camp fire songs. Giant claws snapped at the air, reminding a passing troupe of Spanish troubadours that they needed some fresh castanets.

Plumes of acrid turpentine smoke rose from an exhaust port on the rear of the main body, "Deal with him Lou, he seeks to destroy all that we have worked for. Batter up!"

The code word forced the mechanical monster to bellow Greek vowels in a random order, a metal arm adorned with the average gate attendance of the Icecapades since inception, tore free a hybrid metal bat from its back. With a shimmy and a guttural bark, Gehrig swung the bat and sent Malcolm flying into the wings.

The crowd went wild, some even changed gender and mammal type, scores of newly formed porpoises realised their folly too late, "I think that's a home run," Turk said dryly, milking the attention as much as he could.

A scraping sound akin to a coffin nail abandoning ship came from the edge of the stage, though passing in and out of consciousness, McKindy's grabber claw hauled his battered form across the mirrored floor.

This only served to inflame Lou Gehrig further, and after tooting his displeasure through his rotting nasal cavity, rushed headlong into the crumpled form. Blow after savage blow rained down on the prone man, the crunch of bone and sound of trinkets being smashed asunder silenced the crowd.

Except for one.

"STOP!"

Okay, I'm not entirely sure this is going to work, but your reappearance has girded my flagging courage and loosening top hat elastic.

"Mr Gehrig, your honour, Turk, or whatever he calls himself, has been lying to you."

I really wish people would stop gasping, I've already had a family of four seep into my corded dancing boots, no amount of varnishing or volcanic rubbing will get them out, that's for certain. Okay, I'll just push my way to the front, he's stopped pummelling poor Malcolm, so that's something, though I trust that Turk fellow as much as that disease dealer operating out of the serving hatch of 'Fast Yams'.

I hope Gehrig doesn't start wailing on me, that last batch of Mark was rejected by my bloodstream, I don't think my bone marrow has the appropriate elasticity to deal with a prolonged assault. If worse comes to the worst, I'll plead for clemency, or decant my DNA into that shopping cart caster nut lying on the stage.

"Mr Gehrig, cast your mind back to the day of your incarceration, and to your dearest companion in life. Your spaniel, Scraps. Whilst travelling through the insulation fluid over yonder, I stumbled upon his mangled and burnt corpse. You were promised he too would become a robotic marvel, and that you would both be able to frolic, unfettered, across sun smothered plains once more."

Well that has definitely got his attention, the pressure on Malcolm's throat is easing, that's for certain, the colour is returning to his blood. Don't milk it, but I need a bit more yet, just don't overdo it, or Gehrig will be playing keepy uppy with my enlarged kidneys.

"Remember the days you spent playing hide the penny? The long winter nights when it got so cold and Scraps darned your lucky rabbit's foot in the hope that a better morn would befall you?"

That's it, chatter away to me, he's dropped the bat, so I am taking that as a good sign. Slightly unfortunate it landed on Malcolm's face, but we can sort something out.

"You think I'm making this up huh? Well, as I fought off hordes of twisted sexy security syringes, Turk's private bodyguard I'd like to add, I managed to wrestle free a bone, before they destroyed the evidence, here."

Okay, I thought a one-time pro-athlete would be able to catch, but never mind, this should seal the deal. Yep. His decrepit corpse is thrashing around in that tepid washing up liquid. Wow, he's pissed. I think if he loses any more gaskets he might lose the ability to beat the crap out of Turk.

"As I smote one of the sexy security syringes, they confessed to me that Turk was behind it all, he wanted a stranglehold over you Mr Gehrig, he's been playing you like a fluffer's harmonica for years."

Holy shit, that hit the spot, Lou Gehrig took off Turk's arm with some speed and is administering it to his nether regions with aplomb. "They also said that Turk is more of a cat man, and abhors canines, he said that no one should trust an animal that relies on another to teach it how to lick its own balls."

Awww, he's left the mangled corpse of Turk and has picked up that manky bone I found, and yep…he's crying now. I knew his feelings for Scraps ran deep, but, if I'm being honest, I'm beginning to lose any respect I had for him now. For years, I, and all of the diseased community idolised Gehrig, but to see him brought so low by a stupid dead dog, well…this changes things.

That's a bit extreme, I wasn't expecting Gehrig to tear himself apart, but this could work in my favour. Old maniac taught a lesson, new villain bleeding out into the still not removed fountain of ill repute. I think I'll go and hear his valediction and then see if I can get me some diseases, I'm in severe need of a top up.

Okay, fine, so I feel a little bad for Lou Gehrig, he was a rusty razorblade in a festive game of apple bobbing. In the end that bastard Turk twisted him to his own end and used him as an enforcer in his own fiefdom.

What an absolute dick.

"Tell us what you did with the previous winners Turk, why did you not honour them and mulch them into something truly horrific for mankind? What foul ends did you stoop? What vile pacts did you make?"

Well that's just dandy, he disintegrated them into pipe cleaner, just so he could use them in his central heating? That is certainly unorthodox, still removed the competition I guess, he's been able to run this caper for over a decade now, and no one has so much as raised a crippled eyebrow.

"You must've kept some though, knowing you. If you tell me where they are, I may spare you yet."

Nothing.

This guy, even with both of his arms and his tattoo of the Honey Monster missing, doesn't elicit any sympathy from me in the slightest. Wait an indigo crayon inserted into the moonshine minute…

"Fine Turk, if you won't tell me, perhaps this little fella will help…"

Didn't think I'd be using this Truth Aphid from Stabby on this guy, was saving him for Derrick later, so he can divulge where he's hidden that good batch of DELIRIOUS

WOOTING. Still, if I can get my hands on the remnants of every Gehrig winner since it began, well…I could well come out of this with something akin to Santa's grotto elves home videos.

Ooohhh, the aphid has clamped down on his mammary gland, this should be over quickly. "That's right Turk, you tell me where, and I'll promise that I'll bludgeon you to death with Lou Gehrig's metal toe nail.

Ha, all too easy. I'll honour my agreement, for I am a gentleman. A scholar, a paragon of virtue and decency in this-

Who am I kidding, if I don't kill the bastard, he'll only come back in a sequel, or worse, he'll make some new disease and try and outdo me commercially. Yes, this is a mercy killing, take that you fiend.

Wow, his head came off really easily, I wonder if I'd be allowed to take his skull, hollow it out and use it as a novelty popping candy dispenser? No one to ask, plus, I reckon I could mulch his brain down too and add it to the rest of the previous celebrity winners slurry.

This will keep me going for a few years.

Think of all the wonderful misery and suffering I can inflict.

Now he's gone, Malcolm can-

Bugger.

Malcolm.

"Stay with me Mr McKindy, we'll get you help, you'll be back on your feet in no time."

PROLAPSE

One Year Later

I can't believe Derrick is doing this to me, tonight of all nights, "I said I wanted you to show Cannonball Run this evening." Honestly, ever since he decided to stay as a drive in movie theatre, he's become a bit up his own ass, but he does make a focal point in the bar now, very decent of Jed to turn it over to me, especially after everything that happened.

Well it's award night tonight, Stabby got over the incident and found God hiding in a teapot he had for sale and Laura MacKenzie said she'd be in later. The first McKindy award ceremony for celebrity virology, some say I should've named it after myself, but that is just hubris. Besides, after he passed and I...used his new diseases to set myself up.

I guess it meant that he got to follow through on his promise, plus his pygmy rat fuelled jet-shoes are something else.

"Ladies and gentlemen, a little hush. I know it's been quite the year, not just for me, but for the world of diseases in general. Through my brilliant new range which allow you to experience long forgotten sensations or relive halcyon days. And though I am nominated for the McKindy, I want you to know that should I win, it will be for all of us."

Like hell it will, it's mine, all mine. Once I found a way to reproduce it, with the help of that wizened dodecahedron and gurney spirit, all I had to do was take my rightful place. I was born to do this, it's in my bubbling blistered veins, it beats within my vacuous fur lined chest, and you'll always be a part of it.

To me, and you, oh humble side-effect, we have enough produce from McKindy, Turk and the winners of the Lou Gehrig awards, to last us until the gravy uprising.

Let's go make history.

CELEBRITY CULTURE

103

ABOUT THE AUTHOR

If you looked upon him in the street, you would remark to yourself that Duncan P. Bradshaw resembled a large legume on spindly legs, and blessed with a belly formed from biscuits and beer.

It would only be when he rapped your knuckles; with a yardstick, stolen from the front garden of number twenty-three, (you know, the one with the filthy net curtains and stripped down moped), that you would realise that you were in the presence of a complete and total arsehead.

Yes, he is.

He also writes bios slagging himself off, because much like a bullet with your own name on it, there is nothing you can say to him, that he has not already written down and published.

Now go away.

But do come back. He's needy like that.

MORE FROM

The Sinister Horror Company

Class Three – Duncan P. Bradshaw
Class Four: Those Who Survive – Duncan P. Bradshaw
Burning House – Daniel Marc Chant
Maldicion – Daniel Marc Chant
Mr Robespierre – Daniel Marc Chant
Terror Byte – J.R. Park
Punch – J.R. Park
Upon Waking – J.R. Park
GodBomb! – Kit Power
The Black Room Manuscripts, Vol. 1 – Various

Sign up to our newsletter at

www.sinisterhorrorcompany.com

And receive an exclusive e-book of three short stories

Facebook:

www.facebook.com/sinisterhorrorcompany

Twitter:

www.twitter.com/sinisterhc

CLASS THREE

Hungover, dumped and late for work.

On an ordinary day, one of these would be a bad morning, but today Jim Taylor also has to contend with the zombie apocalypse.

Follow Jim during twenty four hours of Day One, as he and his zombie obsessed brother deal with the undead, a doomsday cult and maniacs in their quest to get to their parents, win his girlfriend back and for them to instigate 'The Plan'.

Worlds will collide and fall apart in a Class Three outbreak.

'This, ladies and gentlemen, is a classic. This is a book that all people who read horror stories need to have on their shelves. Horror. Yes. Comedy. Yes. Does it mix well? Absolutely yes.'
- Confessions of a Reviewer

'Plenty of guts, a shed load of violence, and doused from head to toe in comedy. Absolutely superb stuff.'
- DLS Reviews

CLASS FOUR

Those Who Survive

The dead rule the world.

In the months after a deadly virus has swept across the planet, an eight year old boy and his appointed protector live from day to day. After a chance encounter they head for sanctuary. To get there, they will have to run the gauntlet of the inhabitants of this new world.

Ruled over by The Gaffer, a group of survivors holed up in a derelict factory struggle to maintain order and stability. Inside, those affected the most share their stories, hoping to come to terms with what has happened and what they've lost.

However, a clandestine operative in their midst lays the groundwork for an assault, the likes of which none of them have ever seen or could hope to prepare for.

These are the stories of those who survive.

'The true genius of Duncan P. Bradshaw is the rollercoaster ride of words and expressions. I have never seen an author go from the depths of dark and gore to laugh out loud all within the same paragraph.'
-   2 Book Lovers Reviews

'Class Four is a total blast of a novel from beginning to end and, like its predecessor, is one of the better interpretations of the zombie apocalypse.'
-   Ginger Nuts of Horror

www.sinisterhorrorcompany.com

Lightning Source UK Ltd.
Milton Keynes UK
UKOW06f0411190316

270488UK00019B/543/P